ALSO BY

MASSIMO CARLOTTO

The Goodbye Kiss

DEATH'S DARK ABYSS

Massimo Carlotto

DEATH'S
DARK ABYSS

*Translated from the Italian
by Lawrence Venuti*

Europa
editions

Europa Editions
116 East 16th Street
New York, N.Y. 10003
www.europaeditions.com
info@europaeditions.com

The translator would like to thank
Martha Tennent Hamilton—who paid the price.

Translation by Lawrence Venuti
Original Title: *L'oscura immensità della morte*
Translation copyright © 2006 by Europa Editions

Library of Congress Cataloging in Publication Data is available
ISBN 1-933372-18-4

Carlotto, Massimo
Death's Dark Abyss

Book design by Emanuele Ragnisco
www.mekkanografici.com

Printed in Italy
Arti Grafiche La Moderna – Rome

DEATH'S DARK ABYSS

A pardon is not the reward for a confession. It is an opportunity for clemency which considers the general interest in ending a specific sentence, and only a demagogic confusion of ideas would allow any importance to be assigned to the victim's forgiveness. A pardon concerns the relationship between an individual convict and the exigencies of the law.
The sentence gives the victim all that is his due.

GIUSEPPE MARIA BERRUTI
Judge of the Court of Cassation
(*La Repubblica*, 3 January 2003)

There are avengers who, if science might discover a way, would prolong the lives of criminals for a thousand years and thus enable them to serve out the thousand-year sentence they were given. Besides, has not God already done this very thing by laying the foundations for eternity so that reprobates can suffer the eternal pains of hell?

RAFAEL SÁNCHEZ FERLOSIO

PROLOGUE

1989—a city in northeastern Italy.

The defendant had a split lip, two black eyes, and a broken nose bulging with styptic swabs that stuck out of his nostrils, forcing him to breathe through his mouth. He was being held up by two officers from the penitentiary police who had to help him to his seat. He was a mess. The judge looked at the lawyer, irritated, trying to determine whether he would request an adjournment of the interrogation. The lawyer reassured him with a shrug. His client had plenty of other problems to worry about. Relieved, the judge dictated to the court clerk the personal particulars of those present and asked the defendant if he intended to submit to questioning.

Raffaello Beggiato turned towards the counselor who encouraged him with a theatrical wave. "Yeah," he answered with effort. His mouth hurt. He lost a few teeth when the cops pounded him, and he bit his tongue when they squeezed his balls. But he wasn't about to whine. The beating was part of the treatment reserved for criminals caught red-handed. The intensity varied according to the crime. And his was the kind of crime that authorized anybody who wore a uniform to break his face. While he was at the police station, in the room where they handcuffed him to a chair, bulls from the other departments dropped by just for the pleasure of kicking his ass or spitting in his face. Beggiato didn't get riled by it. Besides, he knew the rules of the game. He only hoped they'd cart him off to jail fast. Nobody would touch him there, and he could concentrate on finding a way out. With any luck, the janitor in the solitary lock-up would be an old acquaintance who'd score

some coke for him. He needed it to get his strength back and
clear his head. But nobody turned up, and the corporal in the
infirmary had refused to give him a painkiller. He'd spent four
hours stretched out on a cot, staring at the bare light bulb that
hung from the ceiling, suffering like a dog and obsessing about
the interrogation. It finally sank in that not even a few lines
would inspire a decent solution.

The judge outlined the case, but the defendant didn't listen.
He knew how things had gone down. He and his sidekick had
studied the job for a couple weeks. It seemed like child's play.
They decided to dress the same and add a touch of originality
to the robbery: they bought two silk balaclavas, the kind motor-
cyclists wear, and two black velvet suits. They'd gotten hold of
the weapons a while ago and had already used them to clean out
a couple post offices along with the registers at three supermarkets. On the appointed day they waited for the jeweler and
his wife to unlock the steel-plated door upon returning from
lunch. They suddenly came up from behind and pushed their
way into the shop. The dealer sputtered the usual bullshit, but
he didn't put up a fight and opened the old Conforti safe without a word. It was crammed with worked gold and top-grade
stones. Jewels new and "antique"—a sophisticated term the
dealer used to cover up a shady pawnbroking business. This
merchandise didn't show up in any register and would be dis-
creetly omitted from the list of stolen valuables.

He and his sidekick took about ten minutes to empty the
bags. Long enough for a police patrol to get there. The wife
had pressed an alarm button they knew nothing about. The
mastermind had sworn there wasn't any hidden alarm, but the
fact is, he didn't check. Never trust guys with clean records
who start committing crimes to pay off gambling debts. They
face life as if it were a crap game, relying on luck and the odds.

They looked each other in the eye. "Fuck the cops," his
partner said.

"Fuck everybody," he said.

The haul was the kind that sets you up for life, and it was worth the risk. Maybe, just maybe, if they hadn't been coked out of their brains, they would've surrendered and minimized the damage. But right then they were thinking at the speed of light, boldly moving in an orbit far beyond common sense.

He grabbed the jeweler's wife by the neck and pushed her out of the shop, aiming his gun at her head. His sidekick had knocked out the dealer and made his exit, carrying the bags filled with the goods. Everybody started shouting. Them, the cops, the hostage, bystanders. They didn't know what to do. A yellow car suddenly wheeled out of a cross street and wound up smack dab in the middle of the mess, separating the good guys from the bad guys.

They made the most of it. After throwing the hostage to the ground, they sprinted for the car and pulled open the door. At the wheel sat a woman, her face twisted with shock; in the rear was a child asking his mamma what was happening.

A few seconds were enough to commandeer the car and take off with the new hostages. Several hundred meters later the car was blocked by back-up patrols. He climbed out with the little boy, threatening to shoot if they weren't allowed to pass. When he was convinced the cops didn't intend to lie down and roll over, he squeezed the trigger. The bullet entered between the neck and shoulder and pierced the body, exiting from the other side. The kid flopped down on the asphalt. For a moment the mother's scream outstripped every other noise.

The cops' jaws dropped. They must've thought he wasn't a professional and didn't play by the rules. Killing the boy wasn't necessary; they just had to sling around some threats, and they would've been allowed to go. Till the next move. They weren't in America, where people get shot at the drop of a hat. This was a quiet city in the northeast, and the body laid out in the street belonged to a blond kid who'd just gotten out of school.

"Now they won't want to deal anymore," was all his sidekick had to say.

Beggiato was wise to him—and knew the guy would get a charge from shooting him in the back. But he still needed Beggiato to make a getaway.

They took advantage of the momentary confusion to take off again, but the cops were everywhere. The woman was ready to cash in. She started swinging at them, shouting she wanted to die. The car skidded, and he was forced to give her what she wanted. A shot in the belly at close range. Then they slipped down a blind alley. The low wall that closed off their path was easily scaled, and his partner jumped to the other side. Beggiato passed him the bags with the take, wasting precious time. Three police cars arrived at top speed. He had no other choice but to surrender or die. He chose life. He threw down his gun, took off the balaclava, and dropped to his knees, raising his hands high over his head.

"The woman passed away an hour ago," the judge informed him. "The doctors could not save her. The child, however, died instantly."

Beggiato said nothing. He'd already taken the woman's death as a foregone conclusion.

"You are a previous offender," the judge continued. "It is pointless to explain what you are facing. The only reasonable course to adopt, if you are seeking any degree of clemency, is to confess your accomplice's name."

The defendant delicately ran his tongue over the stump of a broken tooth. "I wasn't the shooter."

"That is of little importance," replied the judge. "The penal code does not distinguish between material perpetrators and accomplices."

Beggiato watched the lawyer as he began to study the toes of his shoes with particular attentiveness. The decision to squeal or pay for both himself and his partner was his alone. If he decided to talk, his jail time would be decreased, but he'd have to give up his share of the loot—as well as the respect his name had earned him among thieves. And he really didn't feel like paying for his crime with a bad rep. He couldn't get out of this situation cheaply.

He decided to put on an attitude. After all, he'd clocked in exactly ten years as a crook. He removed the swabs from his nose to speak more clearly. "I can't give up that name." His tone was cocky. "If I did, even your honor knows that when I get out I couldn't enjoy my share of the loot."

The judge smiled, satisfied. Beggiato was an utter fool. That statement would provoke indignation and a desire for revenge in the jurors at the Court of Assizes. Before continuing, he made sure the clerk had gotten it into the record, word for word.

"You, sir, shall have no opportunity to enjoy a single euro of the loot. Aggravated robbery, unlawful restraint, resisting arrest, double homicide—an eight-year-old child and his mother. I shall recommend and obtain a sentence of life imprisonment without much difficulty."

The defendant knew the judge had spoken the truth. And without the least exaggeration. That day he'd made a series of fuck-ups. The biggest one was not letting himself be gunned down in the alley. He stood up and asked to go back to the jailhouse. At this point, words had lost their meaning.

When Beggiato left, the judge addressed the lawyer. "Convince him to talk, and I'll recommend thirty years."

"I'll try in a few days. Right now he's in no state to think rationally."

"You're not planning to have him take the stand to sway the court?"

"Don't you worry. If he doesn't confess, I'll withdraw from the case. The crime is hateful, and I don't want to get crucified by the newspapers."

SILVANO

A quick glance at the mailbox before heading home—my routine on week days. Mine was the first in a bank of six gold-colored aluminum boxes, each with a glass slot and a name computer-printed by the condo's managing agent. Right away I saw the lone envelope was a letter. Nobody had written to me in years; just bills and flyers stuffed in the box every once in a while. The lawyer's name, typed in flowing letters, gave no clue. Back inside the apartment I placed the envelope on the kitchen table, slid my meal from the rosticceria into the microwave, and went to change. That day had been a real grind. I resoled and replaced the heels on a rack of shoes. And I duplicated a bunch of keys. Every month started off like this. As soon as people pocketed their pay, they hit the shopping centers to spend it. My shop was planted right in front of the supermarket check-out lanes; it was impossible to miss the sign, "Heels in a Jiffy." The customers dropped off their shoes or keys and picked them up after they filled their carts.

The timer announced the food was hot. From the fridge I grabbed a carton of wine, the cheese, and the utensils. I switched on the TV. I steered clear of the news and surfed for a decent program. Picked a quiz show. A pile of euros if you guessed the right answers. The host was simpatico enough, a guy with a belly; the contestant was a woman, a teacher from down south, thin as a rail. Her voice had an annoying nasal twang. She got eliminated before I polished off the lasagna. During the commercial I opened the letter. I calmly wiped the knife with a paper napkin and slipped it under the edge of the flap.

Dear Signor Contin,

My client, Signor Raffaello Beggiato, has entrusted me with drafting a petition for pardon. The process requires that the parties who suffered loss or injury state an opinion concerning this request. Enclosed you will find a letter in which my client asks for your forgiveness. While I realize that this new chapter in the judicial proceedings can only revive painful memories for you, I urge you to read it with a profound sense of humanity. Signor Beggiato has served more than fifteen years of his sentence. He is now stricken with a grave form of cancer whose course does not seem to offer any hope of recovery. My client's wish is to be able to end his life in freedom. In the hope that you can understand Signor Beggiato's human drama and see your way clear to forgive him, I send you my sincerest regards.

Alfonso De Bastiani, Esquire

My hands were shaking. I took a long swig of wine. Then the quiz show came back with another contestant. A computer technician from Viterbo. I couldn't focus on the question, but the applause from the audience told me he guessed the answer. The host went over the ground rules in the competition, then announced another commercial break. I took the other letter out of the envelope.

Dear Signor Contin,

I dare to make this appeal to you only because I am desperate. I have learned that I am sick with cancer and there is no hope. Up to now I have served fifteen years. I know this is not much for the terrible crimes I am guilty of, but the sickness will put an end to the sentence too. I beg you to forgive me and make a statement that favors a pardon. My only wish is to be able to die a free man. I realize I am asking you to have pity on somebody who stole the dearest objects of your affection. But you are different from me, and you are certainly capable of such a noble gesture.

Raffaello Beggiato

The quiz show came back again. The next question hinged on an episode in the private life of a famous singer. The kind that drives kids crazy. The contestant turned a whiter shade of pale. Gone was his confidence—and his smile. He didn't know the answer. I snatched the remote and turned off the TV.

I read Beggiato's letter again. That fucking son-of-a-bitch murderer was asking me to pity him? I balled up the letters and threw them in the trash. Pity was a feeling that belonged to another life, before death had put mine under wraps. So cancer was killing him: that was nothing but an act of justice. And it was just that Beggiato should suffer to the very end. In jail, obviously. Surrounded by lifers and guards, with no loved ones and no comforting words. His death wasn't going to ease the pain that had ruled my life for fifteen years, invading my time, my thoughts, my daily routines. The pain throbbed like a festering wound, but it made me feel alive and helped me get my bearings in the dark immensity of death. The news about the murderer's fate fired my curiosity. How would Beggiato kick? Over the years I'd learned how to categorize different ways of dying. Some people die in their sleep and never notice a thing. Others pass to a better life suddenly, in the very instant it takes for a thought to form. But this happens only with adults. At eight years old, my son Enrico definitely knew what death was, but he was too scared to be aware of the risk. He heard the shot and felt the burning trail the bullet dug into his body, and his life ceased after a handful of seconds. At least that's what the coroner told me, and when I asked him if my son had enough time to see death's darkness, he rested a hand on my shoulder, rattling off some words that fit the occasion. And yet my question wasn't senseless. I was with Clara when she died in the hospital: she'd seen the darkness.

"Everything's gone dark, Silvano," she said in a loud voice, squeezing my hand tight. "I can't see anymore, I'm scared, scared, help me, it's so dark."

Darkness, fear. Death's dark abyss. Some, like Clara, die after a drawn-out agony. It's the worst way to go. Their facial features get twisted, their limbs shrink. This was the end fate should save for Raffaello Beggiato, the murderer.

I straightened up the kitchen. Then I opened a drawer and took out the photos of Clara and Enrico. They were not mementoes of happy times. Those were buried in the boxes that preserved my former life, stored in a rented garage. The only photos I've kept within reach were shot on the steel table at the coroner's. I studied my wife's and son's chests, cut open and plundered by scapels. The pain throbbed more intensely, and a twinge rose from my stomach to my throat. But the thought of Beggiato's illness helped me dodge my usual tears. That miserable fuck thought I was capable of noble gestures. To forgive you need to have feelings, a life. All I had left was in my hand at that moment.

Once upon a time I'd been a man who was content with his lot in life. I was a sales agent for top-drawer wines. I had a secretary and tooled around in a Mercedes. I had a wife and son. Friends and relatives. Clara was a beautiful woman. I fell in love with her at a party, and we were married in two years. I loved her body and her joie de vivre. Enrico arrived three years later. A sweet, carefree kid. Thirteen years together. Then Enrico and Clara crossed paths with Beggiato and his accomplice, and everything was over. For them *and* me.

That day I happened to be in an enoteca. I was selling one of the prime oak-aged cabernets when my secretary phoned.

"Silvano, hurry to the hospital. Clara had an accident."

In the corridor there were too many police for a simple accident. A doctor told me to step on it; Clara didn't have much time left.

"What happened?"

Excited, overlapping voices referred to a tragic fatality.

"Where's my son? He's O.K., isn't he?"

An inspector's pitiful lie sent me into the intensive care unit, worried only about Clara. I came out asking myself how I was going to get the news to Enrico. Only then did I learn the truth. A robbery, two dead, one criminal in custody, the other on the run.

I retain only confused memories of those events. There were so many people at the funeral. An endless succession of hugs, handshakes, comforting words.

My photo ended up in all the newspapers, along with Clara's, Enrico's, and their murderer's. Everybody in town knew me. I couldn't go anywhere without getting stopped by someone. They all pitied me. Right away I realized I'd have to find another job. I couldn't show up at an enoteca or a restaurant to ply my pricey wines. To sell them you had to smile, crack jokes, make small talk, act like you were sharp and on top of things. But I was the guy whose wife and son had been killed. And my clients would've always remembered it, judging my every word. Anyway, work wasn't a problem. I'd put aside enough cash to start a new business.

My mind was filled with a single thought: the capture of Beggiato's sidekick. The police had no idea who he was, and the murderer hadn't confessed. The idea that he was wandering around foot-loose and fancy free literally drove me crazy. Every day I turned up at the police station. Valiani, the superintendent in charge of investigations, would shake his head, spread his arms, and grumble some stock phrases.

I decided to carry out my own investigation. Through the lawyer who represented me in the proceedings against Beggiato, I got in touch with a private detective, an ex-marshal in the carabinieri. He squeezed me for a lot of dough, and the only thing he discovered was that the murderer had been linked to some whore who worked night clubs, Giorgia Valente.

I pretended to be a john, but she made me right away. Without beating around the bush she told me to stop breaking her balls. That's just how she put it. I threatened to give her name to the papers, and she changed her tune. She told me she knew nothing about the robbery; Raffaello kept her in the dark about his business. She explained whores were considered unreliable in the underworld. Raffaello used to hang out with a lot of people. The girl gave me a list of names I later handed over to Valiani. But none of them turned out to be involved.

The search for the robber stopped me from going to pieces completely. I feared the time when I'd have to face up to the real world. Friends and relatives smothered me with all their attentions. I started avoiding them. Particularly my father and mother. With the excuse of bringing me something to eat, they'd drop by my place almost every day. The house was still thick with the presence of Enrico and Clara. My parents couldn't keep back the tears for more than a few minutes, and I couldn't take on the added burden of their hopelessness.

Around a year later the trial was held in the Court of Assizes. My lawyer tried to strike a deal with Beggiato's new defense attorney: the accomplice's name in exchange for the plaintiff's support of the request for a lesser sentence than life. Nothing doing. The defendant decided to stick to the code of honor among thieves and risk life in prison. Beggiato showed up in a dark blue suit and a flashy tie. He never looked in my direction. But I didn't take my eyes off him. He was a typical thirtysomething; he didn't bear the slightest resemblance to the criminals in TV movies. Didn't look like the kind of guy who'd go out one day, slip a balaclava over his head, and shoot an eight-year-old boy and his mamma. When he was questioned, he gave one-word answers. The presiding judge asked him three times to confess the name of his accomplice. But he kept on repeating he couldn't.

The public prosecutor was relentless and efficient. He asked for the maximum sentence, and I noticed a couple jurors clearly nodding in approval. The defense attorney limited himself to an appeal for clemency; his only argument was the pointlessness of a life sentence when the convict might eventually be reintegrated in society. What a load of bullshit. Everybody in town wanted an exemplary sentence. During breaks in the trial, journalists came up and tactfully interviewed me. Beggiato's mother, a grubby, hopeless woman, chased them away, bombarding them with insults.

The defendant gave a statement before the court retired to chambers. He repeated for the zillionth time that he wasn't the shooter. A judge on the panel shrugged. Idle chatter.

When the presiding judge uttered the phrase "life imprisonment," the people who had followed the trial exploded into unrestrained applause. Beggiato, pale as a corpse, didn't move a muscle.

A journalist stopped me at the courthouse door. "What will you do now?" he asked.

I didn't have the desire, let alone the energy, to start living again. The parish priest urged me to find strength in God. I'd been deeply shaken by his homily at the funeral because of the corny simplemindedness of his remedy: faith will help us overcome the pain of mourning and one day we'll all find ourselves before God who in the meantime loves us and watches over us from heaven above. Amen. I'd abandoned the church many years ago, as soon as I'd finished secondary school. Not for ideological motives or after some episode of internal strife. It was just that religion was foreign to me. I felt ridiculous when I thought of turning to a superior being. That was about it. A cousin who was a psychologist advised me to seek the help of a specialist in order to work out my grief. Everyone, without exception, wanted me to rebuild my life. I didn't even try it. To me their words were empty and false because I didn't possess the tools to confront death rationally. I couldn't seek consolation in faith, and psychoanalysis seemed just as foreign as religion. I was Silvano Contin, the husband and father of two crime victims. The town would've never forgiven me if I picked up the pieces and went back to a normal life. Of course I could've always relocated and tried to start over from scratch. But what nobody understood was that my being had been plunged into the dark immensity of death. How could I love another woman or raise another son with the constant memory of Clara's voice? "Everything's gone dark, Silvano. I can't see anymore. I'm scared, scared, it's so dark."

Those words now beat out the rhythm of my life, dulling colors and tastes. I could only live with my pain in the hope that the other criminal would be caught and punished. His capture wasn't going to improve my existence, but at least the score would've been evened up, and the sense of loss that sometimes kept me from thinking rationally—maybe that'd disappear.

I sold the house and moved to a new, anonymous condominium in the suburbs. Every object that recalled the past I packed away and buried in a garage. Every month I paid the rent on it, but never did I open the door.

With my savings I set up a business in a new shopping center about ten kilometers from the city. The work was easy. It netted a decent income and allowed me to have superficial relationships with customers.

I found it harder to cut myself off from loved ones and friends. Fortunately, my wife's family decided on their own to sever relations. But it was really painful to see my parents, even if I visited them only on Sundays and obligatory holidays. I was their only child; Enrico had been their only grandchild. Banalities alternated with long silences and sudden outbursts of weeping, interrupted by hate-filled rants against Beggiato and his mysterious accomplice. Within three years my parents both died. My father suffered a heart attack at the supermarket, my mother a stroke in her sleep.

As the years passed, my look also changed. I lost hair, put on a few kilos, and started to wear clothes from department stores. I used to shop in the most exclusive boutiques. I'd always go with Clara, she'd make the choices, she had taste. In any case, if someone recognized me on the street, they'd pretend they hadn't seen me. I in turn did nothing to encourage a greeting. I lowered my eyes and shot straight ahead. Embarrassment makes people say the stupidest things.

In the meantime, the murderer's lawyer tried to save his client from life in prison. I didn't show up for the appeal process, not even for the final decision in the Court of Cassation. Beggiato clearly wasn't going to talk, and my lawyer was more than sufficient to represent me. The life sentence was upheld, and the murderer also served three years of solitary confinement during the day, as the court had stipulated.

I kept going to the police station for ages. First once a week, then once a month, until Superintendent Valiani lost patience and told me to stop bothering him. The case was closed. Beggiato was in prison, and his sidekick got away with it. The cops were human beings who did what they could. "All" they could.

For a time I'd also visit the jeweler who was the victim of the robbery. He and his wife gave me a list of the jewelry and helped me put together profiles of their dishonest colleagues, the ones who could've acted as fences. It turned out to be another dead end. The loot had vanished into thin air, like the other robber.

The only person who remained somehow linked to the case was Giorgia Valente, the whore who was Beggiato's girl. I went back to see her quite a few times. Beggiato was writing to her, and I paid her to read the letters. They contained nothing that had any bearing on my investigation. Beggiato seemed resigned, and like every jailbird, he gabbled about sex, talked about jerking off while fantasizing about her ass, things like that. I too hadn't gotten laid in a while. Some nights I happened to dream of making love to Clara. When I awoke, I'd run my hand across the empty bed. I never cheated on her because, apart from the fact that I loved her, she had always been a passionate, imaginative lover. She liked to make love. And she was beautiful. Very beautiful. The whore, however, had a coarse, unattractive face and a body that tended to get fat. Once, when I was reading about the murderer's erotic dream for the umpteenth time, my cock got hard. I paid the whore to fuck her in the ass and then gave her a little extra so she'd write to Beggiato about it.

I never learned whether she did it or not. I don't think she did. Still, from that time on, I kept seeing her once a month—even after she ended her correspondence with Beggiato. I didn't hang with anybody, let alone women. But every so often I needed to get my rocks off, and the ass of the murderer's ex-girlfriend seemed like the best place. In time she got sloppy fat, but for what I wanted to do it was even better. She stopped working in clubs and turned tricks in a studio apartment in the suburbs on the other side of town. I'd phone her, set up an appointment, and amuse myself with her for twenty minutes or so.

"We'll end up growing old together," she once said as she slipped the condom on me, but she never refused my money. Maybe she was afraid of me, or maybe she wanted to make things right somehow. I never asked her. I fucking despised her because she'd been with Beggiato. She was just a warm hole to service my needs.

On other occasions I got spiffed up, climbed into the car, and headed for the city or towns where I'd never been. This was when I'd go to funerals for other crime victims. I'd watch the news on the TV, then find out the place and time, and take off. It was the only moment when I shared something with other people, even if anonymously, even if I really didn't know them at all. I'd sit in the back of the church and stare at the relatives' pain-ravaged faces. I'd listen to the desperate cries of goodbye. Then I'd make a point of standing in line to offer my condolences. I'd squeeze the hands of dazed people who still hadn't realized they'd fallen into an abyss. Before leaving I'd mix with the curious, listen to the comments, feed my pain with platitudes.

The rest of my life was absolutely monotonous and repetitive. I got up, went to work, came back home, watched TV, went to bed. At night I never went out. Never cooked; almost always bought something at the rosticceria. From the day I lost Enrico and Clara, I never drank decent wine. Bought it in cartons. It was just something to help me throw down some food. I'd lost my sense of taste. Everything seemed the same to me, flavorless. The sickly sweet smell of the morgue where I identified my son's body had stayed stuck in my throat. Saturday nights I'd get drunk. Wine and cheap brandy, Vecchia Romagna. When the alcohol clouded my mind, I'd slip on the stereo headphones so I wouldn't disturb the neighbors and dance slow, listening to songs by The Pooh. Clara liked that band. Then I'd collapse on the bed. Sundays I'd get up with a headache, go to the cemetery to put fresh flowers on the graves, and come back home to do the cleaning, counting the hours till I'd be able to go back to work. From the counter of my shop, I could watch people who had real, normal, ordinary lives. I didn't envy them. I was aware my obsession with death had forced me beyond the boundaries of normality, but I couldn't do anything about it. I wasn't to blame: one day mur-

derers had arrived like an invading army, plundering and rav-
aging everything that stood in their path. And the survivors
have to remember and live in utter unhappiness. The problem
was how to fake normality and repress the howl that filled my
chest more and more. "Everything's gone dark, Silvano. I can't
see anymore. I'm scared, scared, it's so dark." I wanted to howl
till I passed out, maybe till I died.

RAFFAELLO

Tomorrow's Tuesday. Another shitty fucking day. Still too many to go till Saturday and Sunday, the best days in prison. Shower, talk, baked pasta, cutlet, potatoes, and football. Lots of football. I bet a Serb two cartons of Marlboro. If Milan loses, I smoke free the rest of the week. That dickhead doctor gets angry about me still smoking, but how the fuck do you get through a life sentence without cigarettes? The inmates that don't smoke, you can count them on one hand. In the yard we had a good hoot at that story about how they want to divvy up the cells into smoking and nonsmoking. These guys at the ministery are real jokers, but have they ever actually seen a jail? Tomorrow's Tuesday. 7:00 A.M., housecleaning. Same routine every other day: a quick lick with a rag and ammonia. 7:30, the breakfast cart comes by. I only have milk. The coffee's crap; the marshal and the stoolies can drink it. My moka's on the burner, ready to go. At 8:00, cell check, doors open, and the janitor gives us the latest news—prison radio. At 9:00, hit the yard. Got to have a one-on-one with that guy in 27; they told me he set up a new ring for weed. Seems like it can help the cancer. And then I got to tell the committee to pick TV shows that ain't so stupid. The afternoon's always torture. I want to see the show with the broads that try to win a date with some numbskull perched on a throne; they're more cutthroat than if they were in court. At 11:30, the commissary clerk comes by. Got to order a shampoo that stops hair from falling out, some toothpaste, and a couple gas canisters for the burner. At noon, the lunch cart arrives. Same routine every other day: pasta, stew, vegetable. At 13:00, the corporal that does the mail comes by. I wonder if Contin got my letter. I hope he answers quick. TV news at 13:30, then catch some z's till 15:00. Another turn in the yard and after cell check at 16:30 the doors are locked. At 17:00, the dinner cart comes by. Tomorrow's Tuesday: minestrone, mortadella, salad. Another coffee to digest and the day's over. The only wrinkles are the cell checks at 20:00, 23:00, 1:00, 4:00, and 6:00 in the morning. If you're sleeping, the fucking screws wake you. And then there's the nurse. That asshole's always late. It's 23:35 and he still hasn't come by. The plastic cup is already sitting on the edge of the peephole. He only has to stretch out a hand and put in the drops. With this business about my cancer, they upped the dose. Better had. The usual dose wasn't doing fuck to me. The shitload of Valium is the only privilege of a life sentence. They're always scared the hopeless might lose their heads and do themselves in. With the tranquillizers they don't have to be on their toes. Fuck, this cocksucker is taking ages. He probably stopped to jaw with his co-workers at the rotunda. What the fuck does he care if we're feeling bad.

Chill out, don't get yourself worked up about being sick. Tomorrow's Tuesday. I'm a guy that knows how to do time and the secret is organizing your day right. The more methodical you are, the more you fuck the system. Night is the real problem. It never passes; you get ugly thoughts. It happens to everybody. The air gets thick with desperation. You breathe the other guys' too. And that fucking nurse still hasn't come by. Another five minutes and I'll raise hell. No, let it slide, that Neapolitan on duty is capable of reporting you, and with the petition for pardon in the works better not look for trouble. I roll another butt. Fucking hell, my throat's dry, and the tap water's cow piss. If somebody asked me what I miss most about being on the outside, I'd answer a refrigerator. I haven't seen an ice cube for fifteen years. I could really go for a stiff whiskey with a lot of crushed ice in a night club filled with entraîneuses.

Just a little longer and I'll be free to drink as much as I want. But what the fuck are you saying, dickhead? You don't have a lot of time. You're dying. O.K., I'm about to die, shit, I'm about to die. I'm fucking scared: I don't want to die in prison. I want to shut my eyes as a free man, even if it's only for one day. And I'll do it. I got a winning plan and for once I'll manage to fuck them. All of them. It was a stroke of genius to refuse treatment in prison. Otherwise right now I'd be at the clinic in Pisa undergoing chemotherapy with no hope of getting out. I decided to risk the disease spreading; it was the only way to play the hand. The request for pardon is just a decoy. They'll never grant it; only my lawyer holds out any hope for it. But he's young and naïve. Contin has no intention of forgiving me, I killed his wife and kid, he'd be crazy to do it, and then this Minister of Justice wants us safely behind bars. So what if some con dies doing life for a double homicide? He ain't going to lose any sleep over it; in fact, he'll gain some votes. The pardon serves only to pave the way for the next move, the petition to suspend the sentence for illness. The life sentence stands and the surveillance judge, who no way feels like having me on his conscience, covers his ass with the press and the ministry. Then as soon as I hit the street, I fetch my share of the loot and make tracks. To Brazil. The doctors say I only got a couple years left; they tell me the last three months are going to be painful, and I'll have to stay in the hospital. I got enough cash to live high on the hog for the remaining time and make sure I get the best care. Down there you just need money and anything's possible. And I'm rich. My partner saved my share all these years. The idea that he might've screwed me never even crossed my mind; he knows certain offenses don't have a statute of limitations.

When I'm cut loose, the nights'll never be like this. I'll be able to stroll along the beach, get laid, amuse myself, maybe even sleep like a rock. In jail, whenever you manage to fall asleep, it's always off and on.

Here the darkness reminds you the red stamp on your file reads, "sentence ends: never." You're fucked. Then you think what a shithead you were to ruin yourself like this. And the memories stop you from getting any rest. Every night I think about that woman and kid. I really don't know how I could've pulled the trigger. But it's done and over with and I can't do a thing for them now. I'm really sorry about it, though. To survive in jail I act hard, but inside I'm sorry for throwing everything away on a life of crime. I could've had a different life. I had every opportunity. I chose to be a crook, nobody forced me, and if it'd been my lot to kill a cop or get plugged full of lead, I never would've thought about killing two innocent bystanders. It's true I was coked out of my brain, but how the fuck did I go and shoot an eight-year-old and his mamma? I ask them to forgive me every night and Sunday mornings at mass. I don't believe in God but I go anyway. It's the only time when the other jailbirds chill out and you can relax.

In Brazil I don't want to have anything to do with the criminal element. The last crime I commit will be going on the lam with a fake passport. I'd rather not do it but I don't have any alternative. With the suspended sentence I'd always risk going back to jail and I don't want to die locked up in a cell in some clinic. If I think about it, I feel like screaming. But I can't do that here. They report you, then cart you off to solitary confinement, and beat the fuck out of you with clubs. Even if you have cancer.

For fifteen years I've been on good behavior in the hope I could use it to get a better deal in prison, get out half days. Years ago you could still hope. Even if you got life. I got ready to toe the line, wasn't going to break out, wouldn't go after my share of the loot. My partner could keep the whole thing. On work furlough you'd have a job, you could start living again, and I would've been satisfied 'cause I'm not the guy I was before, I'm a changed man that has no intention of getting into trouble. But the politicians fucked up the penal reform and now we got ministers—like the current one—who make public statements about our prisons being like four-star hotels. Asshole. I'd like to see his son in here.

At this point very few inmates leave before their sentence is up or with a pass and when they diagnosed my sickness I was kind of happy. First thing that came to mind was, all things considered, it offered me a chance to get out. Then I gave it more thought and finally, when my mother came to visit, I told her to find me a lawyer. My mother. Poor woman. She's my third victim. She's never given up on me. Ever since my father kicked, she's always taken care of me. Now she's sixty-one and she keeps working part-time to make sure I got cigarettes and whatnot. For a stretch I worked too. There was this bicycle factory that hired damn near every inmate but then the cost of our labor no longer made us competitive and now they make the bikes in China. Luckily I still got mamma's money orders.

But when will that motherfucking nurse get here? I'm getting more and more nervous. I can't breathe. Chill, chill, screw this prison, stop thinking about it . . . How the fuck do you stop thinking? For fifteen years I've done nothing but think. The thoughts come on one after another and you can't stop them, can't even put them in order. And you got to keep everything inside; you can't confide in nobody. Otherwise they'll take you for a pushover and use you. Everybody acts hard but they're as desperate as me. Yes, desperate is definitely the right word. I got a life sentence and cancer—what else could I be?

The guard just opened the gate. The nurse's hit this block. Finally. Four cells and he's at mine. Less than two minutes. The time it takes to dole out the drops to the other guys.

Here he goes. Bravo, he keeps holding the bottle upside down. Didn't even look inside the cell. To him I'm just a plastic cup on the edge of the peephole.

One sip and it's done. Night, you bastard, I fucked you this time too. Tomorrow's Tuesday. 7:00, housecleaning. Same routine every other day: a quick lick with a rag and ammonia. 7:30, the breakfast cart comes by. I only take milk. The moka's on the burner, ready to go . . .

"It hasn't even been a month yet, and you're dying to see me?" asked Giorgia Valente when she opened the door. "I've come to give you some news about your ex-boyfriend."

"It'll cost you the same."

"He's sick with cancer. Looks hopeless."

"Sooner or later it happens to everybody."

"He wants a pardon. He's asked me to forgive him."

"And you won't do it."

"I don't even think about it."

"Naturally. Now get a move on, you're wasting time, I got a client showing up in fifteen minutes."

Another letter from the lawyer. Hardly a week has passed, and already he's breaking my balls. "Please forgive me if I press you, but Signor Beggiato's condition is deteriorating . . ."

I phoned the lawyer who represented me at the trial. He told me I didn't have to reply. The process provided that my statement on the motion would be taken by an official. I should expect a visit from the carabinieri.

The Church arrived before the Military. The next morning I found a priest waiting for me at the shop. A thinnish guy in his fifties who seemed sharp.

"I'm Don Silvio, the prison chaplain."

"I bet you want to talk about Raffaello Beggiato."

"He's sick. He doesn't have long to live."

"I've heard all about it."

He ran a hand over his tired face. "I understand your resentment," he said, "and I won't give you the usual sermon about the meaning of forgiveness. But I want you to know something. Beggiato isn't the same man he was before. Prison has profoundly changed him—"

"Fine, then may your God forgive him."

"Within two years Beggiato will be dead. Try to trust him."

"Don't you realize what trash you're talking? Trust Beggiato? Why? He gets out, enjoys the money from the robbery, and dies peacefully."

I lingered over my last words: "enjoys the money from the robbery." I stopped listening to the chaplain. If Beggiato managed to get out of prison, maybe he'd get in touch with his accomplice. He needed hospital care and would certainly try to collect his share if only to secure the best possible treatment for himself. These were no more than hypotheses, but what other means was left to identify his accomplice? No. There was another means. Easier and faster.

The chaplain touched my arm. "Do you feel O.K.?"

"Yes, what were you saying?"

"I was asking you to think about what I told you. If you need me," he said, handing me his card, "you can reach me at this number."

That day I worked without putting my mind to it. After so long I had a real opportunity to discover the other murderer's identity. The real murderer, as Beggiato had always maintained. The snake who killed my wife and son. The ghost who haunted my thoughts for fifteen years. Carrying out my plan seemed like a snap, but in reality it wasn't.

Just before I closed up the shop, I felt ready to make the first move. When I punched in Don Silvio's number, my hands were shaking a bit. He was surprised and pleased to hear from me. We set up an appointment for the following morning, same time.

That night I slept little and badly. I dreamed of Enrico. He must've been two years old. I held him in my arms and sang him a little song that told the story of Croco and Diles.

"I don't know if that will be possible," said the priest, disappointed. Maybe he was expecting an unconditional forgiveness.

"But I have to meet him. It's essential for me to determine whether he's really changed or stayed the criminal I saw at the trial."

"You're right, and I'm very pleased you want to take such an important step. But to obtain an interview authorization is necessary, and it remains to be seen whether Beggiato is willing to meet you."

"If he's changed, he'll undoubtedly want to show it."

"I'll do everything I possibly can to help you. First of all, I'll find out about the procedure and let you know."

When he was about to shake my hand, he changed his mind and gave me a hug. I watched him as he walked away. "Get busy, priest," I thought. "Do something useful for the victims instead of helping the murderers."

After dinner, I switched off the TV and grabbed a pen and paper.

Dear Signor De Bastiani,

Please forgive the delay in my reply. I think you can comprehend the doubts that have made me hesitate before such an important decision. I have not received any news of your client for many years, and his request for forgiveness has taken me by surprise. The illness, however serious, cannot be sufficient to incline me towards forgiveness. What particularly interests me is to know whether Raffaello Beggiato, after fifteen years in prison, has in fact repented of his crime. As I have already indicated to Don Silvio, the prison chaplain, I wish to have a meeting with your client before making a final decision. I want to

look him in the eyes when he asks my forgiveness for killing my
son Enrico and my wife Clara.

Yours sincerely,

Silvano Contin

Now the lawyer got busy too. A week later I went to talk to
the surveillance judge. He was a big fat man with a grey moustache and an abrupt manner.

"I was counting on your refusal to give a negative opinion
about the petition," he began after having me take a seat.
"Beggiato is going to get out anyway, on a suspended sentence
for illness; I'm expecting his lawyer to submit the documents
any day now. But a pardon really seems to me too much for the
crime he committed."

"Perhaps he has truly repented."

The judge stared at me for a moment, then opened a volumi-
nous file. "Beggiato is a model prisoner, never a bad report from
prison officials. But in all these years he's never done anything
to show he's developed a critical attitude towards his past."

"I don't understand."

"His behavior is unexceptionable purely in formal terms.
He has never cooperated with the guards or with prison officials. In short, he's never provided information. He's always
been in solidarity with his fellow prisoners, in the same way
that he protected his accomplice."

"So he hasn't changed at all."

"Precisely. On several occasions he witnessed crimes committed by other inmates, but he was hostile to the investigations. For this reason, I am opposed to granting a pardon. But
if you forgive him, the minister and the president will in all
probability sign the judgment."

"I understand your point of view. But I absolutely need to
know whether he is remorseful for having killed my wife and
son."

"Beggiato will play the part to perfection. He'll succeed in convincing you. I'm quite familiar with inmates. To get out they'd do anything whatsoever. It's extremely easy for them to lie. They're always lying. To the guards, to teachers, to social workers—"

"But he's sick. He doesn't have long to live."

"And for this reason his sentence will be suspended. But if you're determined to meet him, I can only sign the authorization."

"I much appreciate it."

The judge took a form, filled it out rapidly, and signed it. "Don't deceive yourself, Signor Contin. Get ready to be disappointed."

I'd never been in a prison. I was hit by the smell of sweat, food, and smoke, hardly masked by ammonia, and the constant clang of gates brutally opening and closing. The warders looked at me with a certain hostility. They didn't approve of my decision to meet the murderer. They gave me a plastic tray where I put all the objects I had in my pockets.

"The cell phone too," said a brigadier.

"I don't have one."

"You did right to leave it in the car."

Fact is, I didn't own one. I had no use for it. Even the phone in the house stayed silent for months. But I didn't waste time explaining to him. I passed through a couple gates that broke up a long corridor. Then they led me into the visiting room. It was divided in half by a wall about a meter long, topped by a sheet of glass about a meter high. On either side stood benches.

I had to wait about twenty minutes. Then the door opened, and Raffaello Beggiato appeared. He'd aged since the last time I saw him at the trial. He was pale, and his face was lined with deep wrinkles. His lower lip was trembling. He still didn't have the courage to look me in the face. I was worked up too, my hands were shaking, and I had to press them down hard on my knees. I had him right there in front of me, within reach. He was afraid. He ran a hand over his forehead to wipe away the sweat. I decided to make the most of the moment and prolonged the silence. A guard cleared his throat, maybe to remind me the visit lasted half an hour. I noticed Beggiato was wearing a track suit with a hood.

"My son wore a suit just like that when you killed him," I whispered. I didn't want the guards to listen to what I had to tell him.

Beggiato covered his face with his hands. "Please, Signor Contin, it's already so difficult."

He struggled to light a cigarette, but finally got it going. He was trying to find the strength to ask me to forgive him. I didn't do a thing to help him.

"Like I wrote you in the letter, I'm sick, and I'm sorry for what I done. Even if it wasn't me who shot your wife and kid, I feel responsible."

"You want my forgiveness?"

"Yeah."

"Then tell me the name of your accomplice."

For the first time, Beggiato looked me in the eye. "You can't ask me that."

"Why not? You want me to help you get out of jail after you killed my wife and son and I can't ask you nothing in return?"

The murderer burst into tears. "It's been fifteen years, I got cancer, take some pity on me, I didn't shoot them."

"I don't give a fuck about your cancer. I want that name."

"I can't give it to you."

"Then you'll die in prison."

He ran a hand over his eyes. "I don't think we got anything more to talk about."

"Listen carefully. I know you'll try to get out on a suspended sentence for illness, but I'll kick up such a racket the newspapers'll have a field day and the judge'll be pressured to think twice about granting the petition."

Beggiato stood up. "You're asking too much from me."

"Then die in prison, you bastard."

Contin hates me. Wants to fuck me over. Shit, I need something to calm down. That new guy in 14 says he's got some Roipnol to sell. But nobody knows him from Adam. He's Italian but that means diddly. He might be a motherfucking informer and then I'd be in deep shit. You're already in deep shit, dickhead. If Contin gets the papers against me, the minister'll bury me in the clinic. What the fuck can I do? Contin's a son of a bitch but he's right. What if I asked the guy in 27 for a little more weed? He's pricey and doesn't give credit. My stash of cigarettes is gone and the Serb still hasn't paid off the bet. Yeah, Contin's right. I killed his wife and kid and I'm asking for a signature without giving anything in return. But I can't give him that name. First of all, I'd become a stoolie. I could've done that fifteen years ago. Then my entire plan to slip away to Brazil would go up in smoke. I got a right to a little peace. Fuck, I'm dying, it's just a question of time, and these past fifteen years I've suffered like a dog. The doc told me to hurry up and decide about the chemotherapy. The sooner I begin, the longer I can keep the beast at bay. "Aren't you interested in knowing where you have the cancer?" he asked me. "No," I answered. What the fuck do I care where it is. It's there; that's all I need to know. And it eats away inside you like a rat stuffed up your asshole. If I knew where it was, I'd always be feeling that part, I might even start poking around, and that could make it eat into me faster. Then the doc told me I was wrong to keep acting like I was healthy, it's irresponsible. In a different situation I would've socked him in the jaw twice. Could anybody say something more fucking stupid?

Doesn't he know what it means to be sick in prison? The other inmates sniff around you like vultures. Nobody pities nobody here. To top it off, he warned me the pain'd be terrible at the end. Bastard! If I'd been a paying customer, he would've kept his mouth shut. What if I got cancer of the dick? What a hose job! I couldn't have no fun before I kicked. Maybe I got it in the dick for all the times I jerked off. I could ask the Calabresi for a little scag but then I'd have to ask the Bergamosks to borrow their works. Great kids but what do I know whether they've got some fucking disease that'd kill me before my time? They could say the same thing about me, of course. I got cancer and they might not want to lend me their needle. I think I got to pass on shooting up but there's nothing in the cell 'cept cigarettes and coffee. There's no way out; I got to take the risk: I won't give up that name. I'll send a telegram to the lawyer and gamble on the suspended sentence. If it goes south, amen, I'll end up at the clinic. Fuck, could the cops stick me with the damages on the day of the robbery? A bullet is faster than jail and cancer. Much faster. Yeah, I got to bet everything. Maybe Contin won't raise a fuss with the papers. No, he'll do it and fuck me if he does. He's gone off the deep end. But he's right. I'd do the same. I got him wrong; I didn't think a "normal" guy would take it so far. I'll make myself a coffee, just for something to do. When the pain starts I got to be on the outside. With the money I can score some stuff that'll keep the beast at bay. At the clinic they dole out the painkillers with an eyedropper. You're a shitty lifer and nobody gives a fuck if you're suffering. Yeah, I'll send the lawyer a telegram right away and tell mamma to get in touch with my partner. So he can get the money and passport ready. I don't want to get out and then find he's invested everything so he can't hand over my euros. Mamma won't be happy but there's nobody else I can trust with this stuff. In all these years I got in touch with him three times. About three escapes that fizzled out. Nobody breaks out of jail these days. Nobody knows how to keep their mouth shut. I've done my part; now it's up to him. I got to remember to order coffee and sugar. Yeah, I'll do it like this: I'll send mamma and he'll organize my getaway. Provided Contin don't fuck me. He sure has changed. Him too. He's got a face like a corpse, it scares me, and his skin's as white as milk. Looks like he's been in jail. Don't he ever go to the beach? Maybe he's sick. Maybe he's got cancer too. I got to hurry up, in a little while they'll come by to pick up the requests, and I need to get the warden's authorization to send a telegram.

Dear Sir, inmate Beggiato Raffaello, cell 5, second block, requests permission to send the following telegram addressed to his lawyer: I am waiting for an urgent interview. Yours respectfully, Raffaello Beggiato.

How many fucking requests did I make to these bastards in all these years? You want to talk to the priest or the warden or the social worker? Make a request. You want a shampoo that don't thin out your hair? Make a request. You want panettone for Christmas? Make a request. You want to get butchered by the dentist? Make a request. What a great guy he is. He only does extractions for free, 'cause the ministry reimburses him. If you don't want to be toothless at forty-five, you got to pay. You want to pay the dentist? Make a request.

Contin rubbed me the wrong way. I cooked up a whole speech to convince him I'm sorry but he blindsided me. My partner should put up a monument in my honor, no shit. On more than one occasion I was really tempted to sing in order to cut short my jail time. Now more than ever. There was a moment when I felt my legs give and I was about to spill everything to Contin. But then they'd make me testify at the trial. What a fucking disgrace that'd be. If I didn't kill the woman and kid, I'd be proud of myself. But I feel like shit. Never fessed up to anybody about being the shooter. Only my partner knows the truth. And yet every once in a while, like now, I feel the need to tell somebody about it. Don't know why. Before I die I'll call a priest and tell him. Maybe before giving me the last sacrament he'll absolve me from this sin too. Does hell really exist? You don't ask these stupid fucking questions your whole life and then, when you know you'll kick within 730 days, you start covering your ass.

I got to change the ring on the moka. Another fucking request. And the brigadier responsible for outside purchases is a testicle. Most of the time he gets it wrong. I might get saddled with rings for a six-cup moka. It already happened. He's got it easy. When he's on duty, instead of being stuck in the cell block, he tools around the city, buying our stuff, and he still manages to fuck things up. Fuck that asshole pig.

I thought about death and now I'm scared shitless. I feel it in my stomach. I'm fucking afraid to die. When the time comes, will I be conscious? What'll I feel? And then what's going to happen? Will God appear to me, like Don Silvio said, and ask me if I want to live eternally in his presence? Live? What the fuck are you saying, dickhead? What if there's nothing instead? Just darkness. An endless black darkness.

Chill out, stop thinking. Light yourself another cigarette. If I wind up at the clinic it'll be a shitty death. But if I was free I could score some good stuff so I wouldn't suffer and I'd keep my appointment completely unconscious. Then I'd fuck over the grim reaper. Shit, the money. That makes all the difference. It always did. I want to die in Brazil. Like a signore. In the meantime they might discover a new cure and save me. I'll get in a few more years. I'm forty-five, fuck. I'm young. A young lifer. A young lifer with a malignant tumor. And Contin's got the gall to ask me for that name. Up his ass. Up everybody's ass.

Dear Sir, inmate Beggiato Raffaello, cell 5, second block, requests permission to purchase one package of three rubber rings for a one-cup moka. Yours respectfully, Raffaello Beggiato.

I underline "one-cup" so the testicle don't get it wrong.

Superintendent Valiani was surprised to see me. It'd been a while since I showed up at the police station for news about the investigation. He stood up from a desk stacked with files and held out a hand with nicotine-stained fingers.

"Buongiorno, Signor Contin." His tone was guarded.

"I need to talk to you."

"The investigation's been closed for a while now."

"I know all about it. But Beggiato's sick with cancer, and he might get a suspension of his sentence."

"Might."

"I've talked to the surveillance judge: the probability is high."

"So what?"

"Once free he might get in touch with his accomplice."

"We'll keep an eye on him. The fact that we haven't managed to capture the accomplice doesn't mean we've forgotten about the matter. In a couple years I retire, and when I leave I'd like to make a big splash."

"I can relax, then?"

"I'll take care of it personally."

When I said goodbye, it struck me a younger, sharper policeman would've given me more confidence. The accomplice had come back to prey on my thoughts full-time, but at least now his capture seemed within reach. Provided Beggiato managed to get released and then decided to contact him. The fact that the murderer stuck to the code of silence made me think the other guy was still alive, free, and living in Italy, maybe right in this town. Otherwise Beggiato would've felt no qualms about talking. The more I thought about it, the more I was convinced that once he got on the outside, he'd look for his partner. But this time the police wouldn't let him get away. My threat to stop Beggiato's release was just a bluff. Fact is, I couldn't wait for him to get out so he could lead Valiani's men to the shooter. He should be more or less Beggiato's age. He'd die in jail, serving his sentence. Beggiato would precede him. Dead. All of them. The crooks, Clara, Enrico. And sooner or later it'd be my turn.

Don Silvio waited for me to finish dealing with a customer.

"What happened?" he asked me, worried.

"What do you mean?"

"Beggiato's upset. He didn't want to tell me how the meeting went."

"Maybe because there's nothing to tell about it."

"You won't forgive him, then?"

I shrugged and started the machine to file down some heels. The priest gave up after a couple minutes. He said goodbye with a weak wave that signaled defeat.

That evening I found a summons from the carabineri in my mailbox. I went to the barracks immediately. A brigadier in civilian clothes informed me it had to do with the request for a pardon submitted by Beggiato.

"I'm sorry to disturb you with something like this," he said sincerely.

"Don't worry. I was expecting it."

"What do I write? A favorable or an unfavorable opinion?"

"Unfavorable."

The man who was waiting for me at the exit must've been around forty. He said his name was Presotto and he was a journalist. There were three dailies in town. One was center-right, another center-left, and the third was the local supplement of a big national newspaper. Presotto worked for the first.

"We've heard Raffaello Beggiato filed a petition for a pardon," he said. "I imagine you're opposed."

I glanced at his double chin, his olive complexion, the glasses he wore (he was nearsighted). I didn't want to talk to him just then, but he obviously meant business, and I knew I wouldn't be able to shake him off easily.

"Yes, I've just entered an unfavorable opinion."

"Don't you feel sorry for Beggiato? He's got cancer and doesn't have much time left."

Journalists are always like this. One question leads to another. I tried to lie without being self-conscious. "From a human point of view, I regret the state of his health, but the crime he committed is too serious to merit clemency."

"Is it true that you met with him in prison?"

"Yes."

"Was it you who wanted the meeting?"

"Yes."

"Why?"

"I was curious. He wrote to me, asking for my forgiveness. He swore that he'd become a different person, that he repented—"

"But instead?"

"This wasn't the impression he gave me."

"Can you be more specific?"

"No, I'm tired, I want to go home."

"One last question. Today his lawyer De Bastiani filed a petition for a suspension of sentence due to illness, and in all probability it will succeed in gaining Beggiato's release. What do you think of the fact that the murderer of your loved ones will soon be free anyway?"

"The decision will be made by the Court of Surveillance, which isn't bound to ask for my opinion."

"Then you're opposed?"

I didn't answer right away. I had to make a choice between

preventing Beggiato from being released and helping him in an effort to get to his accomplice.

"Let's just say the matter doesn't concern me. Besides, the suspension doesn't cancel out the sentence. Beggiato will still be a convict sentenced to life."

"I'm really surprised," said Presotto, "and a little disappointed. I was expecting a harsher, more determined reaction. Personally I think this criminal deserves to stay where he is. My newspaper has taken a clear political position. I think you know what I mean. It could have been useful to you."

I understood perfectly. I shook his hand in silence and walked quickly away. I didn't want to say too much to Presotto. I didn't know how to act; I was afraid of saying things that might hurt my still murky plan. I hoped I hadn't made any mistakes. Anxiety and unease made me stop in a bar. It'd been a long time since I did that. I ordered a caffè corretto with Vecchia Romagna. The barista was a young foreigner who served the coffee without deeming me worthy of a glance. He kept on talking to the girl behind the cash register. I was grateful for it. I really needed a moment to think.

I used to be able to deal with people. Now I was always on the defensive. With customers too. If someone wasn't happy with my work, I couldn't even justify it and defend myself. I preferred to let them not pay. But this rarely happened. Concentrating on heels, soles, and keys gave me a break from my obsessions. TV had the same effect. Spending hours in front of the screen was essential to wrenching time away from my anguish, although it was a job to find programs that didn't remind me, even indirectly, of my loved ones' violent deaths.

I avoided the news, discussions, crime movies, cop shows. I didn't even follow football. Two Sundays before the tragedy I went to the stadium with Enrico. He had fun and made me promise to take him more often. My preferred programs were quiz shows and ones with singers, comedians, and dancers. I glanced at the news in the papers every morning, before opening the shop. At that hour of the day I was stronger. The most dangerous time was the evening, when I opened the door and knew I'd find no one waiting for me. Then I'd switch on the TV to break the silence of the solitude that could only unleash memories.

With these thoughts on my mind I slid the key into the lock. I switched on all the lights and raised the volume on the TV. Instead of taking the frozen penne al salmone from the fridge, I decided to cook. Broth from bullion cubes and pastina. Something hot to get rid of the acid from the caffè corretto. I set the timer for cooking the pasta. Seven minutes. I added butter and parmigiano. As Clara used to do when she made it for Enrico. That night wasn't going to be so easy.

Presotto's article came out two days later. I had to reread it a couple times. The emotion prevented me from concentrating. Near the title was a photo of Clara and Enrico. They were smiling. Beside it was a photo of the murderer. The serious, indecipherable expression of the hardened criminal. Beneath was mine. It'd been taken at the trial. I stared at my bewildered eyes. They still hadn't gotten used to death's dark abyss.

Raffaello Beggiato Soon to Be Released?

Everyone in town will remember the ruthlessness with which the robber Raffaello Beggiato and his never identified accomplice killed Clara and Enrico Contin fifteen years ago. It was a brutal crime, and Beggiato should have paid for it with life imprisonment. Should have. It seems, however, that the convict will soon regain his freedom because of a malignant tumor recently diagnosed by prison doctors. Technically it is defined as a suspended sentence for illness. It should be applicable only in cases where the discontinuance of imprisonment enables the sick inmate to be cured so as to allow him to serve the rest of his sentence.

Beggiato, condemned as well by illness, should not benefit from it. Yet pity often oversteps the limits of the law, and the surveillance judges tend to interpret the articles of the code with incomprehensible benevolence. Obviously, citizen-inmate Beggiato has the right to receive the best course of treatment. But why set him free when he can be treated in prison? The fact that in all probability he will fail to recover from the cancer cannot in any way soften the rigors of the law. Life imprisonment is the most severe sentence provided by our penal system, and in the case of Raffaello Beggiato it is amply merited.

The murderer's wish is to meet his Maker as a free man. And in fact his lawyer has filed a petition for a pardon. This, however, will certainly not be granted because of the unfavorable opinion expressed by the plaintiff in the person of Silvano Contin. The father of little Enrico and the husband of Clara, who were basely murdered by Beggiato and his accomplice, Signor Contin recently visited the prison to meet the inmate; he wanted to determine whether Beggiato was truly remorseful, as he had declared in the letter that implored the bereaved man for his forgiveness. Signor Contin made a noble gesture that demonstrates how, notwithstanding the terrible tragedy, he has preserved a profound humanity. But he did not grant his forgiveness. Beggiato did not convince him.

Why, then, should he be set free? It is evident that, in his condition, the suspended sentence would be equivalent to granting a pardon. No one wishes to torment a sick man, but why is it necessary to forget the gravity of the crimes that put him behind bars? When citizens are taken hostage and killed in cold blood only to enrich oneself, one also needs to have the courage to pay one's debt to society. Of course, we do not ask Beggiato to demonstrate that he has this courage. But we urgently ask the Court of Surveillance to do so. And we ask the Minister of Justice to continue to demonstrate the resolve that has thus far distinguished his mandate.

Presotto's newspaper had begun its campaign. Beggiato didn't have a snowball's chance in hell of getting out. The minister wouldn't permit it. And so my plan would go up in smoke. I had to resign myself to the fact that Beggiato's accomplice would continue to get off scot-free.

The photo they ran with the article didn't resemble me anymore, and nobody deigned to so much as look at me. That day too I was Signor Heels in a Jiffy.

I felt strange. More uneasy than usual. The events of those days had provoked feelings that altered the precarious balance governing my life. The howl was more difficult to repress. It ripped open my mind with its obsessive rhythm and plummeted straight to my chest. "Everything's gone dark, Silvano. I can't see anymore, I'm scared, help me, it's so dark." I wanted to head home and stretch out on the bed, but it would've only gotten worse. I tried to concentrate on my work. One nail, one blow of the hammer. Another nail, another blow. Then I turned on the machine. Cut, shine, shine again.

"Everything's gone dark, Silvano."

"I know, my love. I know."

The next day the newspaper published another article along with various opinions from readers. Presotto had succeeded in rekindling the city's interest in the case. I read a few lines, then threw the paper in the trash can at the supermarket.

It took two days for me to calm down. In front of the mirror I summoned up the courage to admit I was a wreck, incapable of confronting the changes in a world I'd constructed with so much effort.

Then I received two visits. All of sudden, everything in my life changed. Once again.

The first visitor was an elegantly dressed lady, about forty-five. She reminded me of someone, but I recognized her only after Don Silvio had introduced her. She served as a juror in the trial in the Court of Assizes. She was the third from the left. Then too she was a classy broad, the kind you know comes from the right side of town as soon as you see her. She gave me a warm smile, as she had often done during the testimony.

"Excuse me if I'm disturbing you," she said with a slight Venetian accent. "But after reading Presotto's article I felt it was important to tell you how terribly sorry I am for having supported Beggiato's life sentence."

I looked at the priest with open hostility. "You never give up, do you?"

"Listen to her, please."

"To what end?" I asked, my blood boiling. "I've already given an unfavorable opinion about the petition."

"One can always remedy this," insisted the chaplain.

The woman placed a hand on my arm. "At the time I thought it was just that Beggiato should pay with life imprisonment, but over the years I gave it more thought, and I realized that life is an inhuman sentence. Everyone, even the worst criminals, has a right to a second chance—"

"Bullshit," I interrupted her. "You're another fanatic. A child of Jesus who's afraid to take responsibility. Beat it."

She didn't. She squeezed my arm tighter. I stared at her, dumbstruck. She was a beautiful woman, green eyes, a well-shaped mouth. "I'm not religious," she corrected me with firmness. "After my experience in the Court of Assizes, I became a volunteer in an organization that helps inmates. I've devoted years to understanding my error."

"Beggiato's really pulled one over on you, eh?"

"I've never met him. I visit a prison in another city."

"What do you want from me?"

"A gesture that is responsible. And human."

"That's all?"

"Don't be sarcastic, please."

"Get out of here," I blurted. "Both of you. And you, priest, don't let me see you anymore."

The woman put a card on the counter. "If you feel the need to speak with me, don't hesitate to call."

"I've already got the priest's number. He told me the exact same thing. I don't need to talk to anyone."

She gave me a sad smile and left, followed by the chaplain.

The second visit I received the following night. I found Raffaello Beggiato's mother waiting for me at the door to my building. She was exactly as I remembered her, just older. I was tempted to ask her what she'd done to get hold of my address; my name isn't listed in the phone book. But it wasn't hard to guess she must've gotten it from the lawyer, De Bastiani.

"Beat it."

But the woman just leaned up against the lock. "They'll let him die in prison, now that those bastard journalists have gone and stuck their noses into it."

I showed her the keys. "Let me go inside."

"The lawyer says he'll never manage to get the suspended sentence without a compassionate word from you."

I was fuming. She was making me lose my patience. "I don't forgive your son. I've already put it in writing. Now let me get by."

"I'm not talking about forgiving Raffaello. Just tell the newspapers you're not against the suspended sentence."

I lost it. I grabbed her by the throat and slammed her against the door. "You ugly fucking whore, I can't wait to see your son die. I hope he suffers like a dog."

Signora Beggiato started to scream, scared shitless. I pushed her aside and opened the door. I sat in the kitchen drinking wine straight from the carton. I remembered how, when Enrico did it with the orange juice, I always told him off. I grabbed a glass and filled it to the brim. My throat was dry from tension. And shame. I put my hands on an old woman. I said terrible things to her. It certainly wasn't her fault if her son had become a murderer. Besides, she must've suffered a lot over the years. She was trying to look after him as only a mother knows how to do. I felt relieved nobody had seen us. The neighbors were complete strangers, and I didn't want to become the hottest gossip in the building. The wine calmed me down. I switched on the TV and tried to concentrate on the final questions in a quiz show.

I was sure I'd never see Beggiato's mother again, at least not near my house. But exactly twenty-four hours later I found her planted where I'd left her. She was tense and nervous. With one hand she clutched a pocketbook, with the other the collar of her dress.

"Don't keep this up," I said, staying a good distance away from her. I didn't trust myself.

She burst into tears. "Raffaello told me you want that name," she moaned between sobs. "I know it."

I suddenly felt drained. "Then go to the police and get them to arrest the criminal."

"I'll tell you. If you get my son out."

The surprise left me speechless. But the woman was lucid and ready to deal.

"Tell the papers you're in favor of his release, and I'll help you find the man you've been trying to track down for fifteen years."

"Did your son send you?"

She pulled a handkerchief out of the pocketbook. "No. And he doesn't have to know anything. This is between me and you. If Raffaello finds out, he won't ever look me in the face again. But I have to help him. I'm his mother. I don't want him to die in prison."

I looked around. A neighbor stood at her window, following the scene, but at that distance she couldn't hear our conversation.

"Come on. Let's take a spin in the car."

*

The next morning I took the former juror's card from my wallet. Her name was Ivana Stella Tessitore.

"Please forgive my behavior."

"I wasn't offended, believe me. I completely understand your state of mind."

Empty words. Politeness devoid of reality. Nobody could know how I felt. Least of all her, who felt pity for murderers. I was ready to hang up, but I'd made a deal with Signora Beggiato.

"I'd like to meet you, tonight if possible," I said without giving a reason. It wasn't necessary. I was sure she'd agree without hesitation. In fact, she invited me over to her place. When I got back from work, I showered and put on some cologne. I wasn't used to going out after dinner. The city seemed hostile and strange to me. On a street I used to drive down almost every night before, I saw only some Eastern European kids selling their bodies. They were blond and thin. They smiled at the cars that passed by.

Signora Tessitore lived in a residential area where I once knew lots of people. Pretty townhouses immersed in greenery. A girl about twenty answered the door. "I'm Vera," she introduced herself, squeezing my hand. "Come in, mamma's expecting you."

Ivana Stella wore a dark blue pullover and a skirt the same color. The simplicity was only apparent. The fabric and cut of the clothes were high quality, and the pearl necklace must've come from the best jeweler in town. She had me take a seat on a couch and offered me a premium cognac. Once I would've sniffed it and warmed it in my hands, treating it in the appropriate way. This time I just gulped down a good half of it, as I searched for the right words.

She tried to put me at ease by talking about herself. I learned she'd separated a few years ago and Vera was her only child.

She was independently wealthy, but she made emphatically clear that she didn't do volunteer work because she was suffering from the boredom of the idle rich. When I had enough of her chitchat, I came straight out with it: "I've changed my mind. I'm in favor of the suspended sentence, and I'd like to find a way to make it known."

She didn't say anything for a couple minutes, taking in the news. "May I know why?"

"No. I'd rather not get into it."

"I understand. Forgive me; perhaps it was a stupid question."

"The problem is that I really don't know how to make a move. I need advice. I don't want this act of benevolence to hurt me."

Ivana Stella poured herself another finger of cognac. "I hope I'm equal to the task. Why didn't you turn to Don Silvio or the laywer, De Bastiani?"

"One is a prison chaplain, the other a young lawyer without experience. But you were a juror at the trial, and you know this town well."

"I think you'll be forced to deal with the press. A letter or an interview could be useful, but don't expect to be understood by everyone."

"This is precisely why I want to take the most prudent course of action. I don't want to be beseiged by journalists."

Signora Tessitore once again fell silent, absorbed in thought. Only then did I become aware of the soft music coming from the expensive stereo in the bookcase that lined an entire wall. It sounded beautiful. I didn't recognize it, but it had the power to touch me. It ended almost immediately, and I was tempted to ask her if she'd let me hear it again.

"I think the best move might be a letter," said Ivana Stella, cutting off my train of thought. "Addressed to all three local newspapers to prevent any jealous rivalries over the scoop. In

this way, you can avoid direct contact with journalists and clar-
ify your position without any possiblity of misunderstanding."

"It sounds like a great idea to me. It's been a while since I've
written anything. If I prepare a draft, would you be willing to
look it over?"

"Very willing. Come see me whenever you like."

At the door she gave me a light kiss on the cheek. She barely grazed it with her lips. "I admire you a great deal," she said
in a whisper.

All the way back home I caressed my cheek, trying to repro-
duce the soft touch of her lips.

I had carefully organized all the words in my mind, and in
no time I knocked out a draft of the letter I'd send to the
papers. I could've done without seeing Ivana Stella again. But
I wanted it to get around that my decision had been a hard
choice, made after much consideration. Fact is, it gave me
pleasure to see that woman. She aroused my curiosity, so much
I would've liked to peep on her in her house. Maybe it was
because when I looked at her I could better imagine how my
Clara would've been at her age. I'd give a lot of thought to it,
trying to imagine the wrinkles around her eyes and mouth in
order to drive out the thought of her corpse in the coffin.
Eventually I learned about the process of decomposition so I
could know the state of her body at every moment. I could
never "see" Enrico in the coffin that was sealed in the vault.
The only sharp image I retained of him was the one of his
corpse at the coroner's.

"Is he your son?"

"Yes."

"Sign here, please. I'll fill out the form for the identifica-
tion."

"Grazie."

*

The letter was a page full of bullshit. A handful of words in exchange for a name. But Ivana Stella was moved.

"What beautiful words," she said, wiping a tear from the corner of her left eye with the tip of her middle finger. The nail was painted an elegant red. I took advantage of the gesture to examine her hands; they looked like a young girl's. A sign of high-priced creams and no manual labor. I closed my eyes and sniffed her perfume. A classic with staying power. Clara wouldn't have been so unimaginative. As Ivana Stella continued to read the letter out loud, I stood up to help myself to another drink, and my eyes wandered over her hair and down her back. The elastic from her pantyhose was sticking out from the waist of her skirt.

"It's perfect," decided the murderers' solace. "I can scarcely imagine how difficult it must have been for you to write it."

I shrugged. "It had to be done."

I walked to the door, asking myself whether she'd give me another kiss. Instead she took my hand in hers. "I'm really happy to have met you."

I arranged to meet Beggiato's mother at the entrance to a tobacconist's near the train station. A mailbox was nearby. When I turned up, she was already waiting for me. She looked scruffier than usual; her hair was uncombed and dirty. I was holding three envelopes addressed to the local newspapers. They were still unsealed.

"Here, read," I said in a low voice.

She took one of them and read a few lines to be sure I'd kept my end of the bargain. Then she gave it back to me.

"I'll tell you the name when you put the envelopes in the box, O.K.?"

"I'll keep my word."

Despite everything, she was still hesitating. She was betraying her son. I said nothing. I knew in the end her mother's love would win out.

"Siviero. Oreste Siviero. The address is in the phone book."

It wasn't a particularly unusual name, but hearing it pronounced was like getting an electric shock. The envelopes made a dull thud when they hit the bottom of the box. I started to shake, and the howl filled my chest.

Signora Beggiato was afraid. She began to back away, her eyes fixed on me. Then she turned and ran. I managed to drive the howl back into the dark recesses of my mind. I walked away, muttering that name so many times it finally turned into a kind of hiss. I drove to the police station tormented by a thousand questions. One in particular troubled me: how had he lived for the past fifteen years? Definitely better than me, quiet and happy, enjoying the money from the robbery. I imagined a fat guy with a moustache and a gold tooth that stuck out between his lips when he talked. But maybe he blew it all and now was poor and full of regrets: those people didn't know how to save and build a future. When the cash ran out, they'd go somewhere and make a withdrawal with a gun and a balaclava. That's all it takes. If the police turn up, you grab a couple hostages, and if it comes down to killing them, you do it. "Clara, now I'm going to fuck him but good. Let him have fun till Superintendent Valiani drops by. Are you Oreste Siviero? Yeah, why? You have to come down to the station with us. Can I know the reason? Clara and Enrico Contin. The time to pay up has arrived."

I parked near the bar where the cops from the station hung out. While I was backing in, I saw Valiani exit with some coworkers. The superintendent must've said something funny because the others had burst out laughing. Maybe I also made them laugh when I used to come by and ask about the investigation. Maybe they even gave me a nickname. For them, catching criminals is a job. One case after another. Solved, unsolved. After all, they do what they can without allowing themselves the luxury of suffering for the victims. When another cop dies, it's different. I got wind of this at the funeral for an inspector killed near Grosseto, when they stormed an apartment during a drug deal. A South American trafficker shot him in the face and managed to get away. Wandering through the clusters of people at the service, I heard the other cops swear revenge. Their words were hard and burning like bullets. I never learned how the thing turned out, but I wouldn't be at all surprised if they killed the trafficker in a shoot-out or as he tried to break through a road block.

Valiani would ask me how I'd come by the info. I'd never give up Beggiato's mother. The murderer would find out about it, and he'd hate her. She didn't deserve it. I'd answer "personal inquiries." And that was really the truth. After years of searching, the name finally popped up. If I called it quits when the superintendent advised me to, I would've never hit on it. Still, I hadn't been completely straight with Signora Beggiato. I didn't tell her the accomplice's arrest might delay her son's release. There was no evidence of Siviero's involvement, and the police would have to search for it. In the meantime, they couldn't run the risk of letting the accomplice walk. Besides, after the arrest there'd be interrogations, testimony from witnesses, documents from judges and lawyers. In Italy, justice never moves fast. Who knows how Raffaello Beggiato would react. Maybe he'd defend his partner and try to exonerate him. But it'd all be useless. The investigation would pin the murders on him.

I thought about all these things and couldn't decide whether I should get out of the car. Valiani had already been back in the station a few minutes, and I was still sitting there, thinking, remembering, trying to put that name in the proper context as I held tight to the wheel. My knuckles were white with tension. I stayed like this a long time, till I realized I couldn't go in the station that day. The time to tell the superintendent hadn't yet arrived.

*

Siviero Oreste, via San Domenico 26. And just below, Siviero Oreste, Daniela Cleaners, via Cimabue 115.

A working-class neighborhood, partly rebuilt in the 1960s with those big apartment buildings you see in every city. At that hour of the morning, it was filled with people going in and out of shops. There were also lots of students who divided up the cost of the rent. The science faculties were nearby, and this had persuaded many landlords that university students were good business.

The cleaners sat between a pharmacy and an electrician's workshop. Two windows were papered with colored signs in felt pen, advertising various offers. The writing was clearly a woman's. I took a peek inside. A woman was standing behind the counter, waiting on a customer. Behind her I noticed a curtain. Maybe Siviero was in the back room. I started walking, stopping every once in a while to check out the shops. Just beyond was an African hairdresser that shared the space with a grocery store for immigrants. I retraced my steps. The woman was wrapping a pair of trousers. She had to be the Daniela the business was named after. She was tall and thin with a bony face and straight hair, dyed blond, shoulder-length. She was no great shakes and didn't dress flashy, not at all what you'd expect of a crook's girl. Ordinary. But at least he had a woman at his side. I wondered if she knew anything. Ever since I'd begun watching her, she hadn't stopped a second to jaw with the customers. Her smiling face didn't seem to be hiding any secrets she couldn't confess. Siviero must've been leery about confiding in her; sometimes love ends and turns into hate, and anything can happen. Even words worth a life sentence might escape a mouth. I would've never imagined him opening a cleaners. One night on TV I saw a documentary about Belgian mercenaries. As soon as they got home, bunches of them got into the business of washing people's clothes. A psychologist explained that the need to clean up the blood they spilled drove them to a life among washing machines. It seemed like a load of shit to me. I didn't think it fit Siviero either.

I went to see the house where the robber lived. The neighborhood wasn't far away, just on the other side of the railroad tracks. Via San Domenico was a short, narrow street that joined via Santa Rita da Cascia with via San Bernardino. An area of recently built houses, all exactly the same: two floors, an attic, and a garden. I parked in front of number 26. The house was shut up. The lawn was well-manicured; in the back stood a gazebo in the Tyrolean style and a brickwork barbecue. They must've used it for summer dinners. Steaks, chicken alla diavola, sausages, chilled wine, two corpses on your conscience, an accomplice up for life. Siviero must've thought he was real slick, but the party was about to end. He'd be sporting handcuffs and eating the swill in the slammer. The house was the first thing that contrasted with the image of the unassuming shopkeeper suggested by the laundry. Had to be worth around 250,000 to 300,000 euros. It dawned on me that I wanted to know everything about him. And I wasn't planning to run to the police. I felt different, more lucid, less weighed down with pain. Even euphoric at times.

I showed up at work almost four hours late. The optician who opened a shop next to mine asked me if something was wrong. Nothing like this had ever happened in all the years I'd been there. Even some customers were amazed.

"Had to get some documents," I answered, and the guy took it as an opportunity to complain about taxes and insult the minister of finance.

I started working, but my heart wasn't in it. I wanted to head back to Siviero. Wanted to see him, follow him, spy on his life. When a customer asked me when he could pick up his resoled boots, I told him to come back next week. I knew a pensioner who used to work in a shoe factory and often turned up at the supermarket looking for odd jobs. On many occasions he offered to fill in for me, but I always declined. I wouldn't have known where to go or what to do with a little free time.

I found him in the bar on the upper level. He was drinking a glass of prosecco and chatting with the tobacconist's daughter, a plain girl with a fat ass who dropped out of school to sell cigarettes, candy, and lighters.

"I'm not cut out for studies," she once told me. "Besides, I earn a decent salary here, and the job is secure. Why should I study?"

The pensioner's name was Gastone Vallaresso. He was about sixty-five, sharp and witty.

"I can start right away," he said, enthusiastic. I didn't discuss the pay, but I reluctantly had the drink he insisted on buying me. I couldn't wait to leave. I explained the few things he didn't know and told him to make sure he always gave a receipt.

"How long do you think you'll need me?" he asked.

"I have no idea. A few days, a week."

I ate a sandwich in the car while I kept an eye on the cleaners. Every time the door opened, I had a jolt I wasn't able to control. I couldn't breathe, and my heart pounded. The anxiety was starting to torment me. Sometimes it blurred my vision. The darkness of death seeped past the edges of my mind. "Clara, love," I implored, "let me be." But I felt a mounting wave of desire to go inside the laundry and free the howl.

"Everything's gone dark, Silvano. I can't see anymore, I'm scared, scared, help me, it's so dark."

I murmured it softly as I sometimes did before I fell asleep, when I switched off the lamp on the night table and darkness took possession of the room.

The few men who went into the shop that afternoon were all customers. To see Oreste Siviero in person I had to wait till closing time. First the woman left, heading towards a yellow Smart car parked almost in front. Then a man who immediately turned his back to me to lock the door and pull down the gate. He showed me his profile when he climbed into an SUV that had to cost at least 25,000 euros. He started the engine and left calmly. I stayed right where I was, weeping, my head leaning against the wheel. "I found him, Clara. I found him."

When I reached via San Domenico, the cars were already safely in the garden. The lights in the house were on, and a normal life was unfolding there—talking, the noise of dishes, taps running, the TV in the background. People who were alive, looking at one another, touching one another. It wasn't just that Oreste Siviero should live my reality, what was mine by right. His had been built by destroying mine. That motherfucking bastard in his pretty little house, with the lawn and the barbecue—he was the only one who'd gotten something out of it. Me, Beggiato, his mother—we'd all been fucked. Me most of all.

It was a long night. I couldn't calm down. New scenarios continually took shape in my mind. Triumphant epilogues of justice prevented me from sleeping, but in the morning I didn't feel tired. I was ready to start over.

At seven I again stationed myself in front of the house. An hour later the electric gate opened. First the Smart drove out, then the SUV. They took different directions. Obviously, I followed him. He stopped in front of a bar. Through the window I saw him greet a couple people. The asshole was in a good mood. I got out of the car and went into the place without exactly knowing what to do. Siviero was standing at the counter, stirring a coffee.

"Un caffè," I ordered in a loud voice. Then I slowly turned around to look at him. He did the same thing, giving me a distracted glance I found reassuring. He hadn't recognized me. He raised the cup to his mouth. And I took the opportunity to eye-

DEATH'S DARK ABYSS · 65

ball him more closely. He must've been my age, just under fifty. He had the same build as Beggiato, but he was healthy and in good shape. His conscience hadn't troubled him enough to let his appearance and health go to hell. He had a broad face, a small, fleshy nose, dark, determined eyes, short hair with long, neatly trimmed sideburns. He had on designer clothes, and he wore them naturally. I spotted a Rolex on his wrist, but unlike the hoods on TV he wasn't flaunting rings and chains. Just a thin band on the ring finger of his left hand. He was normal. Like so many other guys. He was with a woman who was like so many other women. His life couldn't have been anything special.

"Ciao, Tosi, see you later," he said in a low, deep voice.

"Oreste, don't forget the points on the pool," said the cashier.

He waved and left.

I looked at the coffee, then the barista: "A Vecchia Romagna, please."

I was acting on instinct. It was too much of an effort to think. I'd found Beggiato's accomplice after fifteen years, and I didn't know what else to do but go with the flow. I went home, grabbed two pairs of trousers and a jacket that had been perfectly cleaned and pressed, and threw them on the floor to get them dirty and wrinkled. Then I shoved them in a plastic bag and showed up at Siviero's cleaners.

The woman was helping other customers. She greeted me with a quick, impersonal smile. I knew it well; I also used it at Heels in a Jiffy. He wasn't in sight; he must've been in the back operating the machines. I tried to steal a glance behind the curtain. No luck. I killed time by getting a better look at the woman. The neckline of her blouse opened onto a small chest. Her hands were cared for, but her skin wasn't as white and soft as Ivana Stella's. Economic differences could be noticed in the little details. Her face revealed the rural origins typical of our country. She had a small scar on her forehead. When it was my turn, she flashed me another smile. I pulled the clothes out of the bag and put them on the counter. She checked them and bent down to write the receipt. This gave me a chance to stretch out my neck and sniff her scent. She smelled of spices and chocolate. A bit vulgar and trendy.

"Your name?" she asked.

Once again it was instinct that guided me. "Contin, Silvano Contin," I said in a loud voice. The woman had no reaction, and this was proof her husband had kept her in the dark about everything. From the corner of my eye I saw the curtain just barely move. I quickly shifted my line of vision. The slit was parted by a hand, and my eyes met Siviero's. The curtain suddenly closed.

"You can pick them up the day after tomorrow in the afternoon," the woman said.

I paid, slipped the change and the receipt into my wallet, and returned to my car, parked a short distance away.

Siviero came out a few minutes later, looked around, then went back inside. After so many years something had shattered his confidence, and he needed to know if the guy whose wife and son he killed had come into his shop purely by chance. He'd seen me a few hours before in the bar, but it wasn't clear whether he recognized me. One thing was certain: from now on he'd pay attention to my face.

After about twenty minutes I saw him come out again and head for a phone booth. He talked a short time, although obviously worked up. He had a peculiar way of gesturing, shaking a rigid hand as if to wave air in his face.

He left his wife the nightly task of closing up. I easily followed him through the city. He parked near the start of a bus route and had to run so he didn't miss it. He got off at the third stop and turned around, eyes worried-looking, hands stuffed into his trouser pockets. I kept behind the bus, which moved slowly in the traffic. Near the center of town I saw Signora Beggiato get off. This is who he'd phoned from the booth. I slammed on the brakes and ran after her. I reached her in an instant and grabbed her by the arm.

"Why'd you meet him? What were you talking about?" I asked.

The woman raised a hand to her heart. "Holy Madonna, what a fright."

I waited for her to calm down, but I kept squeezing her arm hard. I tried to reassure her with my look, but that poor woman was in a tizzy.

"Raffaello asked me to contact Siviero so he'd get a passport and his share of the robbery ready for when he got out. That's how I knew his name. Today he phoned to tell me everything was ready."

"Why are you telling me this? Don't you want your son to get away?"

"No! I want him to stay with me. I've been waiting fifteen years."

"You're playing a dangerous game. Stay away from Siviero. The police are going to turn up soon."

"You're the one who's playing with fire. What got into your head to make you go to the cleaners?"

Nothing had gotten into my head. I just did it. At that moment I thought Clara might be guiding my actions. And right away I convinced myself there could be no other explanation. Clara knew what I had to do. One part of me felt the only sensible thing would've been to knock on the door of a psychiatric hospital and say: "I've got a problem." But another part of me was engulfed in death's dark abyss and couldn't see a thing. It was dark. Pitch dark.

I let Signora Beggiato go, and she walked away, mumbling insults at me.

In the meantime, a motorcycle cop had stopped next to my car and was writing me a ticket. "Did you see where you stopped?"

Half the car covered the zebra crossing. "No. But you're right; I deserve a ticket."

He gave me the once-over to see if I was pulling his leg, but the expression on my face told a different story. The cop tore the ticket from the pad and handed it to me.

"Next time pay more attention," he warned me.

Back home I took a shower. Then, in pajamas, I went into the kitchen to find something to eat. I found würstel in the fridge and boiled the sausages in a pan of water. I ate them with some crackers and red wine. They had a strange taste. I looked at the expiration date on the wrapper. They should've still been good. When I read the label more carefully, I saw they were made from chicken. Chicken würstel? I'd never eaten them before. I thought they were only made from pork. I couldn't get them out of my mind all night. I went to bed asking myself if they ate that chicken crap in Germany too.

I dreamt of Enrico. I was holding him in my arms. His head belonged to an eight-year-old, but his body was a newborn's. He didn't want me to rock him. We stayed stock still till he shut his eyes and fell asleep.

The next morning, as I waited for Siviero at the bar, I read the local papers. They all made the publication of my letter front-page news. The commentary came from every direction. Presotto's article maintained that he understood the great human value of my words, but once again he appealed to the judiciary and the minister to act so that the rigor of Beggiato's sentence would remain unchanged. In accordance with justice. The center-left paper assigned the commentary to an expert who asked why the relatives of victims were entrusted with a decisive role that recalled a tribal social structure more than a constitutional state. The local insert of the national daily limited itself to a point-by-point summary of the case, which they ran with large photos of the protagonists. Living and dead. In the center they placed my letter in italics.

Dear Editor,

I would like your newspaper to give me the opportunity to state, once and for all, my position concerning the request for pardon and the subsequent petition for a suspended sentence filed by Raffaello Beggiato, a convict serving a life term. This man, with an accomplice who remains unknown, killed my wife and my eight-year-old son after taking them hostage in the course of a robbery. For these most grave crimes, he was given the maximum sentence provided by our legal system. Fifteen years after the events, inmate Beggiato, seriously ill with a tumor, asked for my forgiveness. After meeting with him in prison, I decided not to grant it for strictly personal reasons that I do not intend to make known. Regarding his request for a suspended sentence, however, after a long and painful deliberation, I believe it to be appropriate to make public my favorable opinion by means of this letter. Even if it is not binding on the judicial decision, I feel it is right to communicate my thinking. Raffaello Beggiato is seriously ill with no hope of recovery, and his death will not give me the least bit of comfort. The pain from the loss of my Clara and my little Enrico will remain unaltered. But this does not prevent my conscience from siding with an act of humanity. To let Beggiato die in prison would be pointlessly cruel, and I hope this does not happen because it would be revenge, not justice. Besides, the suspension of the sentence for illness does not cancel out the crime, and Beggiato would remain, to all intents and purposes, a prisoner sentenced to a life term. I hope that Beggiato, should the petition be granted, might utilize his freedom, not only to undergo treatment, but to reflect with serenity on the terrible crimes he has committed in expectation of the Lord's judgment.

For my part, I ask only that I be left to my pain, which I do not intend to share with anyone ever again. Least of all do I wish to transform it into news or spectacle. We relatives of innocent victims deserve only silent respect.

Silvano Contin

Ivana Stella was right: the letter was perfect. I didn't make a fool of myself, and it enabled me to avoid journalists in the future. Above all, it helped me to find Siviero. Through the window I saw his car pull up a few minutes later.

When he rested his elbows on the counter, waiting for his coffee, I materialized at his side.

"Un caffè, grazie."

The sound of my voice made him turn, and our eyes met a second time. He blanched and suffered a moment of confusion, uncertain whether to take off or to act as if nothing had happened. At this point, he must've realized I wasn't there by chance.

"Remember me?" I asked. "Yesterday I brought clothes to the cleaners."

Siviero didn't answer, but he managed to articulate a sound that could've resembled a yes. He drank his coffee without putting any sugar in it and quickly moved over to the cashier. At the door, he turned back to look at me. I waved goodbye.

I was disappointed. Siviero was such a normal guy that he was quaking in his boots. Armed and protected by the balaclava, he could rob and kill, but in the end he was just like everybody else. It was obvious I had enormous power over him. The mere sight of me must've conjured up terrifying words in his mind, words like police, life sentence, prison. I think he would've done anything he could to avoid catastrophe. That was it. Before sending him to prison for the remainder of his life, I had the chance to make him understand the meaning of pain, anguish, loss. Then he'd understand the rest.

I don't fucking believe it. When the commissary clerk showed up with the newspapers and told me, "There's a letter from Contin in your favor," I thought he was diddling me and I'd already decided to pass on the urge to slash his face in the shower. But it was all true. Shit, that crazy bastard Contin wrote me an A-1 letter. Now I'm sure to get the suspended sentence. Hey, Brazilian chicas, get ready and spread your legs wide. Here comes old Raffaello with a cock as hard as steel. I'm already feeling better. Fucking aye; you wait and see how I beat the fuck out of this cancer. Great day, even though it's Friday. Today fish, the usual hake casserole with potatoes, boiled like the screws' balls. Tomorrow's Saturday, fortunately. I'll have a talk with mamma, who'll give me the good news about the passport and the cash. It's really true, I'm already feeling better. Yeah, I feel "alive." I can't even think about freedom. I dreamt about it so many times and now it's within reach. As long as the lawyer gets cracking and that asshole judge sets a date for the hearing. They already got all the documents. Cancer, cancer, cancer. And of course they can't invent shit. They even got Contin's favorable statement. And that counts, you better fucking believe it counts. I could've sworn he wanted me to die in jail but he wrote: "To let Beggiato die in prison would be pointlessly cruel." What a nifty way to put it. That's reason enough to whoop it up. Seeing as how I'll be on the outside in a little while, I can let myself splurge. Two cartons of Marlboros for a decent taste of scag. I'll mainline it and have a dreamy afternoon. Especially since there's not a fucking thing on TV worth watching. That guy they caught with the payoffs told me on Fridays people do their own thing so they don't bother investing in interesting programs. I can start counting the days that stand between me and freedom. Today when we hit the yard, I'll start divvying up the things I'll leave behind to avoid any cutthroat rivalries. I don't want to see some dickhead wearing my bathrobe. What if they make me do another test and find the heroin? Who the fuck cares. I can say I used it for therapeutic purposes. That'd be a scream. You're getting back your good spirits, Raffaello, keep it up. I really don't understand that Contin. Who knows what he's thinking.

A word crossed my mind like a flash of light: blackmail. I thought Clara might've suggested it to me. I gave into the urge to look up the definition in an old dictionary from secondary school.

Blackmail: *coercion based on threats, practiced against a person with the aim of extorting money or favors or of compelling actions or behavior contrary to a person's will or interests, esp. to blackmail with the threat of compromising revelations . . .*

This is exactly what's going to happen to Siviero. Blackmail will be the weapon of my justice. Bit by bit I'll strip away the life he's stolen from me. And he'll wind up in prison anyway.

I'd never blackmailed anyone, but I didn't feel I needed a plan. I just had to make things clear to Siviero. Then, as Clara always used to say, one thing would lead to another.

"Your clothes aren't ready yet," said the woman behind the counter at the cleaners.

"I want to talk to your husband."

The woman swept back the curtain. "Oreste, there's a customer looking for you."

I heard Siviero's voice ask who it was. She turned towards me.

"Silvano Contin." I said it real clear. "Your husband knows me well."

The man came out of the back room. He was wearing a blue smock so he wouldn't dirty his designer clothes.

"What do you want?" he asked, his tone hard.

"Let's have a chat."

He took off the smock and nodded at the door.

"What's going on, Oreste?" asked the woman, worried.

"Everything's fine, Daniela. I'll be back in a minute."

He led the way on the sidewalk for about twenty meters. Then he suddenly turned around: "So what do you want?"

"It took me fifteen years, but I finally found you."

"What are you talking about?"

"You know damn well. A robbery, two dead, a convict up for life, an accomplice who's been free too long."

"I still don't understand. If you think I've done something wrong, why don't you tell the police? Maybe you're just suspicious and don't have a shred of proof."

Siviero was sly. He was sounding me out to see what I knew. "I was looking to make a deal," I shot back. "But if this is how you want to play, I can go straight to Superintendent Valiani. I really don't think you'll get the passport and cash to Beggiato. He'll be put out by the way you handled this."

He looked as if he'd been cold-cocked. It was enough to see his lower lip quiver to know I had him by the balls.

"What kind of deal are you talking about?" he asked, cagey.

"You're the crook. You should know better than me."

"We should have a sit-down and talk it over calmly."

"You're right. Invite me to your place for dinner tomorrow night."

"My wife doesn't know anything."

"That's your problem."

"It's best not to complicate things. You and I can reach an agreement."

"I can't think of anything more complicated than doing life. Can you?"

He shook his head, beaten. "See you tomorrow at eight then," I said. "And don't get any crazy ideas. You won't get anywhere if you try to take me out. You follow?"

The next morning I was laying for Siviero outside his house, just to make sure he wouldn't make a getaway. During the night I was convinced he'd do it. He already had a passport and the cash he was planning to give his sidekick. Criminals like Siviero are used to being on the run. But the two of them came out like every morning. I followed the SUV to the bar and then to the cleaners. I waited about ten minutes before I went into the shop. The woman was behind the counter as usual. Her eyes were puffy like she'd been having a good cry.

"Oreste!" she shouted, scared when she saw me. Luckily it was still early, and there weren't any customers.

Her husband came out right away. I smiled at them. "I've come to pick up my clothes." Siviero went into the back, and she got busy looking for them, her hands shaking. I grabbed the pair of trousers and pretended to examine them closely. "The crease isn't perfect," I said. "Maybe they need another press."

The woman covered her face with her hands and started whimpering.

"See you tonight," I said as I opened the door.

At eight on the dot I rang the bell at the house on via San Domenico. Siviero-Borsatto was printed on the nameplate. He met me at the door. He didn't say a word, just invited me to follow him with a nod. I entered a large living room filled with expensive but tasteless furniture. Over the fireplace hung an oil portrait of the woman in a wedding dress, as if she might be a countess in some important family. On the facing wall was an enormous TV, one of the latest models. A door led to the kitchen. The wife appeared. She was wearing a tracksuit and department store slippers.

I chewed her out. "You don't receive guests dressed down like that. Go put on some proper clothes."

The woman rushed up the stairs as if I'd threatened to whip her. Siviero dropped into an armchair. He lit a cigarette.

"I didn't think you smoked."

"I started again last night."

"You've got a cute little nest."

"I can give you 250,000 euros. Half of Beggiato's share."

"How is that possible? The jeweler declared a smaller amount."

"A bunch of stones wasn't registered. The shop operated like an underground pawnbroker."

"You think Beggiato'll agree to split the money with me?"

"He'll have to put up with it."

"You want to buy my silence with a share of your partner's money. And you don't put a cent into it? That won't do. Besides, it's too soon to talk about money."

A grimace of resignation was traced on his mouth. "I guessed as much. So you're not just interested in money?"

"No."

"What then?"

"You had a good time over the past fifteen years. Now it's my turn, don't you think?"

"The important thing is to move quick and reach an agreement that's clear-cut and final."

"I'm in no hurry."

I heard the noise of heels coming down the stairs. Daniela had gotten dressed, combed her hair, and put on some make-up with a shaky hand. She was wearing a grey sleeveless dress, short enough to show off her legs. They were thin and straight, sheathed in black stockings. She had on a pair of stiletto heels the same color.

"That's better," I said. "Now I'd like an aperitif."

The woman headed for the kitchen, tickled to leave the room. She came back a little later, carrying a tray with three glasses, a bottle of prosecco, and some tidbits. I hadn't drunk prosecco in fifteen years. Apart from the bubbles, I didn't taste it at all.

The woman sat next to her husband.

"What did he tell you?"

"Everything," he answered.

"He's different now," said the woman, her voice broken with emotion. She had a hard time getting out the words, but she was determined to finish her speech. "Ever since then he hasn't done anything bad. He's gone straight. Take the money, take whatever you want, just leave us in peace."

"In other words, you're on his side." I blew up. "You defend him, and you'd stay with him, even though he's told you he killed a woman and an eight-year-old."

"He wasn't the one who shot them. It was the other guy."

"Beggiato says just the opposite, but it doesn't matter. Your Oreste's going up for life anyway, and you'll make all the papers. 'The murderer's sweetheart.' Is this what you want?"

"No."

"Then from now on keep your mouth shut. I don't want to hear any more of your bullshit. Get into the kitchen. I have to talk to your husband."

The power I had over these people went right to my head. My imagination had no limits. As soon as I'd come up with a request that would make them suffer, I felt I could push it further. But I had to stop the thing from becoming psychologically unmanageable to Siviero. And to do that, I had to make him believe I intended to bargain.

"I want all the money. You tell me where and when, and I'll show up for the meeting with Beggiato. In the meantime I want free access to this house and your wife."

Siviero jumped to his feet and clenched his fists, ready to let one go. "You can't ask for that."

I slammed my hand against the table. "Don't you ever talk to me with that tone. You understand, asshole?"

"Watch you don't cross the line. Otherwise you'll fuck everything."

"Fucking is just what I want to talk to you about. I've been fucking Giorgia Valente once a month, Beggiato's ex. I guess you know her. A whore who goes for fifty euros a pop, fat and ugly. Daniela's nothing to brag about, but she's sure better-looking. She definitely isn't as beautiful as my Clara. If you didn't kill her, I wouldn't be here wanting to fuck your wife."

"The answer is no. I'd rather go to jail."

"Call her. Let's hear what she has to say."

The woman came out of the kitchen. "Don't bother. I heard everything. I'll go to bed with you, Signor Contin. The important thing is for this business to be over fast."

Siviero squeezed her hard in his arms. "Don't feel you're obligated to do this."

The woman twisted free from his hug in a fit of anger. "Shut up, Oreste. Don't say anything. It's all your fault this is happening."

"Excuse me if I don't stay for dinner," I said calmly. "But it looks like you've got to straighten out a few things. I'll be back tomorrow morning around ten."

Siviero escorted me to the door, and the look he gave me when he closed it I didn't like at all. Pure hate. I had to stay alert. I imagined the thoughts forming in his mind like an army of cockroaches scrabbling on their backs. They were furiously working their legs, but they couldn't get themselves right side up. Just as Siviero was racking his brain to find a solution, a way out that seemed acceptable. But there wasn't any. Or, to be more precise, he could either give in to the blackmail or kill me. But in neither case would he get off without a scratch. The idea that he might take me out didn't scare me; I considered this a risk that had to be faced by anybody who administers justice. And as an injured party I had every right to mete it out.

I got my first results. Relations between husband and wife

would never be the same. Siviero had built their marriage on a lie, and now the broad not only had to face the reality of living with a double homicide, but she was forced to pay part of the bill to save him. Well, she chose to take his side. Despite the truth. The man she married had killed a child and his mamma, and she was ready to spread her legs for a perfect stranger to prevent her husband from going to prison. So much the worse for her.

The next morning, before I went back to Siviero's house, I drove by the cleaners. The shop was open, and he was helping a few customers.

I parked in front of the driveway at the house. The woman's Smart was in the garden.

Daniela was dressed like the night before. She led me into the living room without once looking me in the face.

"Make me a coffee."

I followed her to the kitchen and sat at the table. "Why don't you have children?"

"We tried, but they didn't come."

"How'd you meet him?"

"I used to do manicures at the barber shop where Oreste would go."

"You knew he was a robber?"

"I heard some talk."

"In other words, you knew. And you married him just the same?"

"I loved him then, and I still do now."

"Even though he's ready to pimp you out to avoid going to prison?"

"It's no big deal," was her comeback. "I used to give blow jobs in the rear of the shop for extra cash. Anyway I'm only doing it for him. At forty-three I couldn't deal with the consequences of his arrest. I'd lose everything, the house, the shop, respectability. Going to bed with you is really getting off cheap."

"How did it make you feel to find out your husband killed an eight-year-old kid and his mamma?"

She shrugged. "Oreste says it wasn't him who did it. He insists Beggiato flipped out and started shooting for no reason. And I believe him," she said as she poured the coffee into a cup. "Besides, it happened so long ago. Like I told you yesterday, he's different now. He was a petty crook who lucked into something much bigger than he ever expected, and this changed him. He's sorry for what he did."

I felt the rage rising from my stomach to my brain. My eyes filled with spots, and I was worried about feeling sick. This broad was really more than I could take. She was utter shit. "He's sorry? So far I haven't heard him say a single word about my wife and son."

The rage turned into an icy desire to do some harm to her. I drank the coffee in one gulp. "Get up to the bedroom, quick."

Daniela left the kitchen and went up the stairs. The room was at the end of a hallway. The bed had been made. I tore off the spread. The sheets were fresh. She kept her arms pressed tight to her body. I moved away from her and headed towards the dresser. I opened the drawers till I found the one that contained her underwear. I started tossing things to the floor, panties, bras, stockings. I found a sheer negligé, pearl grey, and a pair of thigh-highs the same color. I threw them at her. "Put them on."

While Siviero's wife took off her clothes, I opened the built-in wardrobe and threw everything in the air. Then I trampled on the clothes and started to kick them around. When I stopped, I saw her standing at the foot of the bed in the negligé and stockings. She was afraid. I made her get on the bed on her hands and knees. I undid my trousers and fucked her in the ass. At the beginning she tried to break away, but when I shouted to stop it or I'd call the police, she sank to the bed and didn't make a move. When I came, I grunted in disappointment. Too fast. This fucking whore hadn't suffered as much as she deserved.

I went downstairs and threw a chair at the big TV on the wall. I trashed everything that happened to come within my reach. The oil painting over the fireplace was last. I took it down and stamped on it. Then I left.

I felt frustrated. Siviero's woman bowed to the blackmail, but she struggled to preserve her identity. I gave her a nasty fuck in the ass, but to her it was just the price she had to pay to cut her losses. Nothing compared to the devastation in my life, the pain and anguish I'd known for the past fifteen years. To her and her murderer husband I just represented a problem they had to solve. Then life would go on, even if it wasn't the same as before. The difference between me and them lay right here. My existence had been closed off forever by the dark immensity of death. My present and future were merely time spent in the lobby waiting for the end because I had nothing else. But they could still see light and hope. Even Siviero, once in prison, would continue to see the light, hoping till the end that he wouldn't have to serve out his sentence. And if things went bad at the trial, there was always the appeal and the Court of Cassation. Only I lived forever plunged in darkness.

I shut myself up at home to think. The carton of wine, a cup, and the photos of Enrico and Clara stretched out on the coroner's table.

Hours passed. When I was sure I'd made the only decision possible, it was already dark. I didn't switch on the lamp. The howl was filling my chest, and I was scared the light would unleash it.

RAFFAELLO

Everything's going according to plan. Mamma confirmed my partner's already got the money and passport and my lawyer told me the hearing in the Court of Surveillance will be held the day after tomorrow. He gave me all kinds of advice. "Don't say anything, answer only when questioned, think before opening your mouth, don't look at the judges, always keep your eyes lowered, you have to give the impression you're gravely ill." Then I looked at him like he was an idiot and pointed out that I *am* gravely ill. His answer was I should make it plain to the judges. The judges. There's only one judge in that court plus the public prosecutor. The other people are shrinks and social workers. They look you up and down like you were some sideshow freak so they can justify their salaries. I know all about them. I'm fucking sick and tired of having conversations with experts. Everybody wants to reform you but finally they do what the judge says. I hate them more than the screws. They show up here with their heads full of the shit they learned from books and the sincere desire to rehabilitate you and help you reintegrate yourself in society. But when they see jail is one big lie and every inmate—with no exception—has to lie to survive, the experts change their tune. First the believers who turned out to be wrong are disappointed and don't give a fuck anymore. The women get pregnant so they'll have the least possible contact with scum like us jailbirds and the men ask to be transferred so they'll be closer to their towns. They've got "Who gives a fuck?" written all over their faces. The distinguished experts of the Most Honorable Court of Surveillance really just pretend to be experts. They pose as big deal professors but they don't know shit from shi-nola. It's so easy to do a court job. Most of them never set foot in a cell block. Motherfucker, whenever I think about these things, I see blood. They make you live in a shit hole while the people who should be running the show are robbing the place blind. An accountant who killed his mother-in-law used to help out in the administration and once he let me see some papers. It came out that at least one TV was broken every day, along with tons of light bulbs and other shit like that. All that stuff wound up in the screws' homes. Not to mention the meat. We never saw the best cuts. All the same, the circulars from the ministry clearly state the meat's got to be choice grade. It's a conspiracy hidden behind a badge or ministry ID. And then the people in the Court of Surveillance examine you like you came out of a model prison. They know how things are but they just don't give a fuck. As long as their salaries are secure. The more inmates there are, the more hearings they have to do. They've got overtime pay coming out the wazoo. I've already been there twice to talk about an early release. If you act right, they cut two months' jail time off every year. Even with us lif-ers. It only pays off if they put you on work furlough after thir-ty years—but that's definitely a payoff. They've never given it to me 'cause it was "premature," but I remember the experts staring at me like it was yesterday. I could've kicked them in the teeth till they cried for mercy. The day after tomorrow I'll be an altar boy and won't tell them to go fuck themselves. The important thing is they grant me the suspension and then off to Brazil to die the way I fucking want to die, far from these shits. I've already seen guys die in prison. A Venetian doing a twenty-year stretch for dealing coke had a heart attack. He told them he felt sick but by the time that cocksucking nurse got there and that other cocksucker, the doctor, ordered the trans-fer to the hospital, the Venetian was as good as dead. The screws fucking joked about it and you could hear them laugh-

ing all over the prison. But we didn't say a word. You couldn't
hear a fly in the cells. Dying in jail is the worst thing that can
happen to you 'cause they even abuse your corpse. There's no
pity. Better to pop off between a whore's thighs or OD on heroin or coke. Motherfucking bastards. Hey, kid, chill out. Don't
get worked up. In a few days those prison doors are going to
swing wide open for you. Yeah, 'cause even if everything turns
out dandy the Most Honorable Court of Surveillance won't
issue the order immediately. No, signor. It always takes a few
days because they're swamped with work.

I don't know what's bugging me today. I've got this beef.
Yeah, it's true I'll get out in a few days but it's been hard to put
up with all this corruption and I'm in no mood to take any shit
from these motherfuckers. A sentence on top of the sentence.
Jail isn't just time. It's everything else you got to take and it ain't
written down in the sentence. I shouldn't have let myself get
arrested that day. Before getting plugged with a nine caliber I
might've killed one or two of them and I'd be remembered in
the underworld as a guy that had balls. Instead I killed a
woman and a kid and everybody sees me as a fucking moron
that went off his rocker. Something I got to do is make sure I'm
not identified after I die, got to set something up with a cre-
mation outfit. I want to be gone forever. No trace of Raffaello
Beggiato must remain. I'm making coffee jailhouse style. You
whip up the first drops with sugar till it forms a thick cream.
Then the rest of the coffee streams down real slow so it doesn't
go flat and looks just like an espresso from a bar. Then when
you drink it you realize it's fake. Like everything else inside
here.

I answered on the sixth ring. I haven't gotten phone calls for years, except from ballbreaking surveys or some business that absolutely wanted to inform me about the promotions for their products.

"It's Ivana Stella Tessitore."

"Buongiorno."

"Am I disturbing you?"

"Not at all."

"I passed by the shop, and the gentleman who is taking your place told me you won't be at work for a few days. I wondered if by chance your absence might be connected to the publication of the letter."

"I'm just worn out. The emotional stress . . . you understand."

"I do understand, perfectly. I'd like to see you again. Perhaps a little company would do you good."

"I'd love it."

"Then why don't you come over for lunch today? My daughter is at the university; we could have a chat in peace and quiet."

The prisoners' benefactress sought my company. I didn't much care for listening to her rubbish, but at the same time I did want to see her again. She still made me curious, and meeting her for lunch was one more opportunity to scope out her life.

On my way to her house I passed by the cleaners. Through the window I saw Daniela waiting on a couple customers. She was smiling and chattering away. That whore was really thick-skinned.

Ivana Stella was elegantly dressed and carefully made-up. She welcomed me with a big smile. "I'm really pleased to see you," she said, kissing me on both cheeks.

She parked me in the living room and offered me an aperitif. A Negroni. She'd made a carafe of it. I took a look at her glass and saw she'd already had one. That gave me something to think about. The first time I'd been to her house she helped herself to that premium cognac—twice. And when I came over to show her the draft of the letter, she also had a couple drinks. My eyes searched for the cognac among the bottles that stood on a large round tray of antique copper. Just a couple fingers were left. So the consoler of murderers, thieves, and drug dealers didn't hold back on the alcohol. A weakness that hid some rough patches deep down. That woman had everything. Wealth, a beautiful house, a daughter. And she even allowed herself the luxury of helping inmates. I suddenly stood up, grabbed the carafe, and filled her glass. It was her third.

"This Negroni is really good," I said with a smile.

The table had already been set. For two. Plates, glasses, cutlery, napkins—everything was the height of refinement. Ivana Stella had good taste. The meal had been cooked by the maid who'd gone out a while ago. I methodically filled her glass. A Friulian white wine with the antipasto and a light red with the codfish.

The woman drank and talked. I listened and made free with the reassuring smiles.

"Drink up, cara. I'm guessing you'll pour out your soul any minute now."

And the fact is, in a little while she asked me if we could drop the formality. Then she started telling me about her loneliness. Her husband had left her for a younger woman. Although not more beautiful, she was careful to add. She was all on her own in that big house with a daughter to raise. Fortunately Vera turned out to be a girl with a head on her shoulders. Ivana Stella had been so traumatized when her husband left that she couldn't build a life with another man. Later she met a friend, a woman who worked as a volunteer in prisons, and she found a new reason to live.

By the end of the meal, two bottles of wine had been emptied, but I'd drunk very little. Ivana Stella started to slur her words and repeat herself. I offered to make coffee. In the meantime, I told her I admired her a great deal for her dedication to her fellow man, and I got a kick from making her blush when I asked how a beautiful woman like her hadn't found another guy to share her joys and sorrows.

"Tell me something about yourself," she said as she sat on the couch.

The fool liked hard luck cases, and I was a prime example of the species. All I had to do was mouth a few platitudes, and I won her over. She started telling me how impressed she was by my capacity to understand Raffaello Beggiato's drama and how she'd like to become my friend. She was pathetic, weak, defenseless. She sure wasn't made of the same stuff as Siviero and his wife. I would've been stupid not to take advantage of her. She deserved it. And she might come in handy later.

"I shall be most honored to become your friend too," I said as I stood up.

"Are you going?" she asked, disappointed.

"Yes, unfortunately. I have things to do. But I hope to see you again soon."

At the door, she gave me a big hug. "I'll phone you tomorrow," she promised.

At home I read the newspaper. The next day Raffaello Beggiato was going to appear before the Court of Surveillance. The time had arrived to make another visit to the Siviero couple. I waited for them in front of the house.

"Have you come to smash up everything else?" Oreste asked, barely repressing the impulse to jump on me.

"Down, boy," I commanded. "It belongs to me. I'll do what I want with it."

Daniela ignored me. She opened the gate and parked the Smart in the garden.

"You've got Beggiato's money and passport here in the house?"

"I'm not some idiot."

"Beggiato gets out in a matter of days, and he'll contact you," I said. "You set up a meeting at night to hand over the money and passport and then tell me where and when. That day I'll come by here in the morning to have some fun with your wife. You arrive at lunch time with the bag, and I'll disappear from your lives."

Siviero had a long look at me. "I hope so," he sighed.

RAFFAELLO

That motherfucking attorney general was against it. "It would be pointless to grant the suspension of sentence insofar as Beggiato cannot be cured." Luckily my lawyer did a stand-up job. He fished out an affidavit from some big-deal professor at the University of Padova who maintained freedom could have a beneficial effect on the cancer. And then he wanted to read out the letter Contin published in the papers but the presiding judge wouldn't go for it. "It has already been included in the proceedings," he said, and you could see his balls were twisted. I followed the lawyer's advice to a T, kept my eyes lowered, even if every once in a while I snuck a peek at the faces of the fucking experts. They were staring at me like dimwits. But I was sly as a fox, didn't get up their assholes. And then those fuckhead guards. They used the life sentence as an excuse to play Rambo and clap on the handcuffs so tight they hurt like hell. But I didn't make a peep. Felt like crying from the pain, but didn't give them the satisfaction. So in a few days I get out and hightail it to Brazil. I'll cross the French border by train and then in Paris get on the first flight. If the passport is good there shouldn't be any problems. These days the bulls're only after Muslims. I'm a paleface with light eyes. I only hope nobody fucks me out of the bag that's filled with the cash. But that won't happen. Thieves don't rob colleagues. There was a time when prison guards were carabinieri. Those young bastards were utter pigs. But sometimes you'd find a head guard that'd go to the bar and get you a caffè corretto. In the old days. Now the screws call themselves the penitentiary police but they always have an inferiority complex 'cause they don't do anything but open and close gates and then they act like bastards just so they'll get noticed by the real cops. While I was at the hearing the mail guy came by and left a letter for me on the peephole. It isn't from the lawyer and my mother never writes to me. I still haven't read it. First I'll eat something. Today pasta with sauce, stew with potatoes, and apple. In jail they always give you the short cuts of pasta. It's been fifteen years since I ate spaghetti or tagliatelle. By the time they get it from the kitchens to the cell blocks it'd turn into paste. The short pasta is overcooked too but at least it don't turn into shapeless pap. The sauce is acid, as usual, and they mixed bread crumbs with the grated cheese. So the brigadier in the kitchen can take home a nice piece of parmigiano. But he needs to give some of it to the inmates that work in the kitchen; otherwise this shit don't flush. They're the guys that make prison bearable for themselves. At least they eat well. And inside here food is like drugs. Helps you get through the day. I asked to work as a cook too but the warden told me prisoners convicted of murder couldn't work in the kitchen or the infirmary 'cause they might get the idea to cut or poison somebody that gets on their nerves. Maybe some fat asshole screw. The potatoes've melted and the pieces of meat are as hard as marble. Fuck, Raffaello, how much of this slop d'you eat all these years? Now I'll read this letter. I'm curious as all hell.

Dear Raffaello,
It's been quite a few years since I wrote to you. I'm back in touch just to say I hope you get out and manage to get better. We had fun once, and it's a nice memory I still hang on to. I'm working from home now, and one of my steady johns is Silvano Contin. I'm really happy he decided to write that letter to the newspapers. I'm sure it will help you. I wish you all the best.

Giorgia

Giorgia Valente, the choicest piece of ass in the Veneto clubs. And my old flame. But what the fuck am I saying? She stuck with me only 'cause she hoped she'd live la dolce vita. She was just a whore like the rest of them. Still, I liked her. She knew how to have fun. She wrote to me for a definite reason; if not, she wouldn't go to the trouble. And the message has got something to do with Silvano Contin. The heartbroken widower is fucking my ex. So what? I figured that bastard would go off his rocker, at the very least, what with all the shit that happened to him. Should I be offended? I couldn't give two fucks. Maybe Giorgia's trying to tell me to stay on my toes? Why should I? As soon as I get out I beat it to Brazil. This letter belongs in the trash. Now I can finish off the stew. But I'll cook the apple with a little sugar, real slow, till it gets almost like candy. Shit, the gas canister for the burner's almost empty. Just enough left for a couple coffees. O.K., I'll eat it raw. An apple a day keeps the doctor . . . on your ass. Fucking shit! With my cancer I should be eating a ton of apples. Fuck me, I lost my taste for it. And fuck Giorgia Valente too. How old is she now? Forty-four, forty-five. She's got to be turning tricks at home now; her ass must be scraping the ground. With all the money Contin's got why isn't he fucking whores twenty years younger?

I phoned Ivana Stella. Her daughter told me she'd gone to a prison with the other volunteers. I asked her to do me the favor of returning my call.

I stretched out on the couch to review my little speech for the bleeding heart of the prisons. After a short while, I dozed off. I dreamt of Clara. We were talking to Enrico's teacher. He was saying the boy was the best in the class, but he was so sick. The phone woke me up.

"I wanted to hear your voice. And see you." I went on the offensive.

"Me too."

"But maybe that isn't true."

"Why?" she asked, alarmed.

"Can I be frank and direct?"

"Please."

"I feel attracted to you, but I don't want to make you uneasy. You're a very beautiful woman, refined, intelligent, sensitive. But I'm just Signor Heels in a Jiffy. Once I was successful, but then tragedy—"

"Silvano, I too feel a strong attraction towards you, and what you do doesn't matter to me because you're a special man."

"You're special too. When can I see you again?"

"You could come over now, but some friends of Vera's are here. Is lunch tomorrow O.K.?"

An invitation to lunch, so the daughter won't be there. And at lunch she can drink a little more because Vera mustn't be real happy that mamma hits the bottle. I was put off by Ivana

Stella's affected ways, the "you're a special man" crap. I was special, but not in the sense she imagined. I was finally exercising my right to justice. The judges had also invested me with this power by treating my statement on the theme of forgiveness as a decisive factor. But I didn't forgive anybody. Not Beggiato, Siviero, Daniela, Ivana Stella. Certainly not her. No "volunteer" had shown up to help me when I was groping blindly, engulfed by the darkness. Much less Signora Tessitore who came to the aid of poor inmates. And now she found me special.

Life is weird. For fifteen years I waited for something to happen, something that might give meaning to my pain, and now I was acting completely within my rights. And God was definitely not pulling the strings. God doesn't exist, I'm sure of it. Beyond life there's nothing but death's dark abyss.

Late in the afternoon I was laying low near the cleaners. Shortly before closing Siviero headed downtown on foot. He went into a bar and started shooting pool with some other mugs of his ilk. That night he wasn't going home for dinner. I retraced my steps, got into the car, and passed by Ivana Stella's house, then Daniela's. I finally went to a place that was deserted at that hour of the night. I walked for a long time between mounds of loose earth. The silence gave me a feeling of peacefulness. Only the howl smothered in my chest produced a muffled, broken noise like the planks on a storm-tossed ship.

The prospect of another meeting had gotten Ivana Stella all worked up. And she must've drunk at least two Negroni. When I slipped my tongue in her mouth, it felt like I was licking the bottom of the glass. She answered the kiss like a house on fire. I could've taken her to bed right then, but with a woman like her it would've been a mistake. Everything in its time. Now was the moment for words.

"Life is really extraordinary," I said. "I would've never imagined that I could fall in love again."

"I've thought about it ever since the first time you came over."

"I would like to devote my life to your happiness."

"Oh, Silvano, hug me again, please."

For a good hour, we kept saying the kind of stupid stuff kids say to each another, trading kisses and caresses. Ivana Stella started to get bolder. She wanted to make love. It was then that I gently pried myself loose from her embrace.

"Not now, my love."

"But why?"

"I want to be sure about your feelings. In a few days I'll phone you again, and you can tell me if you truly want to continue seeing me."

Her eyes filled with tears. "I was right. You really are special."

I pulled into a service area on the highway to eat a sandwich. Then I proceeded to the shopping mall just past the toll booth. I carefully chose the things I had to buy and stood in line at the cash register. I didn't have enough money on me, so I paid with a debit card.

That night at home I received a phone call from Don Silvio, the prison chaplain.

"I wanted to inform you that Raffaello Beggiato will be released tomorrow morning," he announced solemnly.

"I am pleased."

"God will reward you for what you have done."

I hung up, embarrassed by the man's gullibility. He had dedicated his entire life to an illusion.

The next morning I waited for Siviero outside the usual bar. "He gets out today," I told him. "I'll phone every two hours to see if he's contacted you. When you hear from him, tell him to keep his eyes peeled. Superintendent Valiani will have him tailed."

RAFFAELLO

The beautiful thing about a suspended sentence is nobody checks up on you. You don't have to go to the police station or expect visits from the bulls. You can go anywhere anytime—you just can't cross the border. The lawyer hammered this point to make me understand it wouldn't be kosher for me to skip the country. Who gives a flying fuck. He got paid. 'Nuff said. It ain't like we're partners. I took a taxi to mamma's place. It would've been great to stop downtown and take a stroll but everybody knows when you just get out of prison you shouldn't overdo it. Too much freedom all of a sudden makes you flip out. Mamma's happy, does nothing but look at me and cry. Fixed me a nice lunch but I can't eat much. As soon as I went into the kitchen I opened and closed the fridge door at least fifty times. Then I grabbed some ice and had a big glass of vermouth. The only booze I could find. That's all mamma drinks. I might go out later and get a whiskey at a bar. The phone rings all the time. It's those fucking journalists wanting to interview me. "How do you feel? Does the cancer hurt? Do you think you'll meet Signor Contin again before you die?" Motherfuckers. I got to avoid them like the plague. Today the dailies printed photos fifteen years old; I'll be fucked if they take new ones of me. I'd be recognized on the street and that's the last thing I want. I won't even look out the window just to stop some dickhead from immortalizing my handsome face as the sick lifer. Fuck, I can't believe I'm free. I still have the stink of jail on me. During the taxi ride I kept my nose glued to the window, acted like a kid 'cause it's one thing to see on TV what's outside of jail and another thing to see it with your own eyes. The city's changed, the people've changed—all these fucking cell phones—the cars ain't the same, the bulls are different too, and the place is crawling with them. Now even traffic cops pack guns. What really turned my head was seeing so many blacks and Arabs walking the streeets. I thought they kept them all in jail. There's always so much Italian snatch. This is the important thing. I'd love to dick a couple of them before moving on to the Brazilian babes but I think I'll have to pass. Time flies and I got to cross the Atlantic and settle in before the cancer saps my strength. Now it dawns on me I've thought of everything 'cept mamma. I didn't even tell her I'm going to Brazil. I'm thinking it's best not to tell her; otherwise she'll lose heart and do everything she can to keep me with her. I'll just vanish and kiss tomorrow goodbye. Leave her a little cash so she don't have to work as a maid anymore. Poor mamma, she'll take it hard but what else can I do? I got to tell her some bullshit story about needing the passport in case they want to put me back inside; that'll chill her out. Yeah, that's what I'll do. In a couple days I'll cut the cord. Tomorrow night I pick up the stuff and then hop the train for Paris. Plus they're expecting me at the oncologist's for the chemo. I want to get cured in Rio with nurses that sashsay to a samba beat. Not with medical benefits where they treat you like some bum off skid row. Besides, in a blink they'd know I was a con that got life and they'd treat me like shit.

After lunch I'll use the excuse of a coffee at the bar and phone my partner. I got to say I'm looking forward to seeing him. It won't be for more than a moment 'cause you never know about the bulls but I want to give him a hug.

SILVANO

To get the key to turn in the garage door I had to spray the lock with a lot of oil. The door opened onto my past. Everything that belonged to Clara and Enrico was stored there. Against the left wall stood a huge wardrobe filled with my wife's clothes, shoes, bags, jewelry, trinkets. Against the right wall stood a smaller one with my son's things. Even his toys were packed away in large boxes.

I sat on the ground with my back up against Clara's wardrobe and began to speak softly to her. I didn't want Enrico to hear.

RAFFAELLO

I still can't put prison behind me. I walk around like I did in the yard when they'd let us out to get some air. I'm always looking at the clock, amazed the cell check didn't happen yet or the meal cart's taking so long to dish up the swill. I can't get used to the money; I know zilch about these fucking euros. I went into a shop to buy some clothes and the salesgirl treated me like I was some fucking Martian. I *am* a Martian. A Martian convict. I talk like a jailbird, always use the same words, and I can't stop myself from slipping a cuss into every conversation. Once some shrinks from the university came to study our language. One of them was a cute chick, even if a bit up in years. She told me "in total institutions the lexicon is reduced to the minimum needed for communication." I didn't understand a thing she said but her cleavage was so burned into my memory I jerked off to it in the shower. Anyhow, I wanted to tell her we didn't have fuck all to talk about, aside from the usual bullshit. We definitely didn't rap about philosophy or history. Inmates only talk about crimes, trials, football, women. The shrink was fascinated by our foul lingo. "Do you realize that for the most part you use coarse language?" How should I talk in jail? I answered, trying to be polite. Then I explained the difference between cock and prick, between crap and piece of shit. Important differences. You couldn't make mistakes on the inside. Finally I told her the guards and the warden talked the same way. Of course, they only did it with us inmates. But that was the language in prison; we ain't in a monastery. What a dickhead you are! You think you're still in jail. You're free and don't have any time to waste. Death is really scaring the shit out of me now. In lockup, every now and then it seemed like a way to beat my sentence but now I feel like I'm sentenced to death. I feel like I got a time bomb up my asshole. Cancer ain't nothing but an enormous cock that fucks you till it kills you. Shit, I'm starting to get depressed. I need to get off. They told me some Albanians're selling Turkish heroin in Piazza Martiri delle Foibe. Where are the Italian dealers these days? I don't trust these Albanians; even in jail they'd always try to fuck you over. Let me make a phone call first and then I'll look for something to distract me.

"He's contacted me," said Siviero.

"I'll be right over."

Twenty minutes later I walked into the cleaners. Daniela signaled me to go in the back. Siviero was smoking, sitting on a metal chair.

"Tomorrow at midnight on the corner of via Don Bosco and via Don Pessina," he said.

"I'll see you at your place tomorrow at lunch time. Don't show up empty-handed."

"And you remember the deal: out of our lives forever."

"I'm a man of my word."

I went back home and phoned Ivana Stella.

"When I dialed your number, my hand was shaking," I lied, larding my voice with emotion.

"Why?"

"I was afraid you might have changed your mind."

"No, my love. I can't wait to hold you again."

"Would you like to come to my house tomorrow after-noon?"

"Certainly. Would four be all right?"

"Perfect."

I slept well. A deep, dreamless sleep. After a shower, I shaved very carefully. Used scissors to clip a few hairs that stuck out of my ears. Dug up an aftershave I hadn't used in ages.

Siviero, meanwhile, looked a mess. I watched him as he got out of the SUV and went into the bar. I followed him to the

cleaners. When the first customer showed up, I started the car
and headed to his house.

Daniela didn't say a word when she saw me set a long, narrow canvas bag on the floor.

"Un caffè?" she asked in a bitchy tone. She was wearing the
negligé and stockings from the last time. The stocking that covered her left leg sagged around the knee. On her feet were
some ridiculous high-heeled slippers. The only trace of make-
up was her trashy lipstick.

"Not today," I answered, taking a look around. The TV I
destroyed had been replaced by a smaller one. The painting
over the fireplace had disappeared. "I want you to take a
bath."

She shrugged. "Whatever you like."

I watched her fill the tub and pour in a huge amount of bath
foam. Then she stripped and got in. I closed the door and went
through the other rooms. One of them was not too big, fur-
nished with a single bed, a night table, and a chair. It fit my
purposes. I moved the furniture to the back and went downstairs to get the bag. I unzipped it and removed several large
plastic drop cloths, identical to the ones used for paint jobs. I
spread out one on the floor; the others I attached to the walls
with packing tape.

"The water's getting cold," said Daniela, annoyed, when I
came back to the bathroom.

I handed her a robe and led her to the room. When she saw
it covered in plastic, she tried to back out, but I pushed her
inside.

"What's all this about?" she asked, frightened.

From the bag I grabbed an axe handle and hit her in the
knees. She fell to the floor, and I kept on swinging till she
passed out. I examined the bruises. It still wasn't enough. I
stood up and took aim. Knee-caps, shinbones, thighbones.
They broke one after another. I sat down and waited. After

almost an hour she opened her eyes and started to moan. I bent over her.

"Did you see the darkness?" I asked.

"Mamma, help," she murmured softly.

I pulled her by the hair. The rough move awoke the pain. She opened her mouth to scream, but she didn't have the strength to do it. "I asked you if you saw the darkness."

She looked at me, her eyes blank, lidded. "Help, call for help, please."

I hit her in the chest with the tip of the stick, gauging the force so as not to kill her right away. I sat down again and waited. She came around a couple times, but didn't say anything about the darkness. She sought her mamma's comfort. I'd read that soldiers in war, when they're in agony, call for their mothers. She never mentioned her husband. A little before one I sat on the couch in the living room. Siviero arrived a few minutes later, holding a leather suitcase. He placed his house and car keys in a bowl. Habitual, routine gestures. I did them too.

"Daniela?" he called in a loud voice.

"She's in the bathroom."

He laid the suitcase on the table. Showed me the money. It was in dollars.

"And the passport?"

He took it out of a side pocket. It was made out to a certain Pietro Andrea Bertorelli. The photo was missing.

"At least give that to Raffaello. It's a copy of a real one. It'd stand up to any inspection."

"Which one of you shot my wife and son?"

"It was Raffaello," he answered, trying to be convincing. "We were wired from coke, and he flipped out." Then he looked towards the stairs. "Why doesn't Daniela come down?"

"She's in the bath."

"I'm going to see."

As soon as he turned around, I hit him in the back of the

head with a sock full of euro coins. He collapsed on the floor,
out cold. I went to get the axe handle and smashed his back,
right at the top vertebrae. Loaded him on my shoulders and
carried him up the stairs to the landing. Then dragged him by
his feet into the room. I brought him around by splashing cold
water in his face. The first thing he saw was Daniela. He tried
to get up to help her, but his legs didn't move. Only his arms
and chest had any life in them.

"You killed her."

"Not yet. I wanted you to see her die."

"You're fucking crazy," he shouted with all his might.

I slapped Daniela to wake her up. She started moaning again.
"Did you see the darkness?" I asked for the umpteenth time.

She said something, but I couldn't hear because Siviero
started to shout. "What fucking darkness? Leave her alone and
call a doctor. She doesn't have anything to do with it. Save her,
I beg you."

It was right then that the howl got free. "Everything's gone
dark, Silvano. I can't see anymore, I'm scared, scared. Help
me. It's dark."

I howled and howled and raised the stick over my head and
let it fall on their bodies. In the end, when silence returned,
there was nothing but blood. I listened to my heartbeat, my
breathing. The howl was gone. It had disappeared. My chest
felt light.

I stripped and threw my clothes on the sheet that covered
the floor. Went into the bathroom to take a shower. Pulled a
change of clothes from the bag and put them on calmly. Ivana
Stella wouldn't get to my house till four.

I detached the sheets from the walls and very carefully
wrapped up the corpses and the axe handle, using packing
tape to seal the openings. I dragged them down the stairs to the
garage door out back.

Then I grabbed the keys from the bowl and left.

*

I stopped in a bar and ate a salami and cheese sandwich. With a glass of red wine. In an enoteca I bought two bottles of an excellent white wine and a bottle of cognac to quench Ivana Stella's thirst. A hefty bill I paid with the debit card. I kept forgetting to withdraw some cash.

When I got home, I took another shower. At that hour, nothing interesting was on TV. To kill time I glued supermarket coupons in the booklet. By this point I'd collected so many of them, I could get an immersible mixer or a hairdryer. I leafed through the catalogue, searching for a more interesting prize.

Ivana Stella had just been to the hairdresser's. She greeted me with a light kiss on the lips. She was embarrassed: she was entering a man's house for the sole reason of having sex. I made her comfortable and offered her a glass of cold wine at the just right temperature. I noticed she was looking around.

"This is the home of a single man. It would take a woman endowed with good taste to transform it."

She took this as a cue to inspect the house and make suggestions. Shades of paint, wallpaper, tile, furniture. When she went into the bedroom, she remarked that the brass headboard was a little out of fashion.

"But the mattress is new," I said, embracing her from behind.

She asked me to lower the blinds. "Do you prefer the darkness?"

"No. Just this time. I'm afraid you won't like me."

I helped her undress. When she undid her bra, she stiffened. Ivana Stella required patience. I was tender and careful. Then I penetrated her and made her come.

We held each other for a long time, mixing sweat, kisses, and senseless words. I got up twice to bring her a drink. Cognac. After sex she preferred it to wine.

She looked at the clock. "It's time for me to go," she said with a sigh.

"Don't you want to take a shower?"

"That would be great. Thanks."

While Ivana Stella got washed, out of curiosity I rummaged through her handbag. I wanted to stick my nose into her business. In her purse I found her daughter's photo and a slip of paper with a silly, ungrammatical love poem signed by someone named Antonio. He must've been one of her beloved inmates.

"Was it good for you?" she asked at the door.

"Very good."

"It's the first time I did it since my husband left."

From the window I watched her get into her little Mercedes. A happy expression was stamped on her face. "Enjoy this moment," I thought. "It won't last long."

I left the house a little later. Parked at the train station and took a taxi to the area around via San Domenico. The Siviero house was immersed in darkness, and the entire neighborhood was deserted and quiet. You could only hear the dogs bark when I walked past them. I opened the gate, drove the SUV around back, and struggled to load the corpses into the rear. Shut all the windows to give the impression they'd left and grabbed the leather suitcase with the dollars and the passport.

I drove slowly to the dump I visited a few nights before. Slipped between the mounds of trash to reach the one I'd already chosen. Dug a ditch, not too deep. Wasn't necessary. Every day the municipal sanitation trucks would unload tons of trash.

I left the SUV near a hotel where taxis were always waiting. The driver put the suitcase in the trunk.

"Coming or going?" he asked without a trace of curiosity, just to make conversation.

A good question. I mumbled something incomprehensible and climbed in the back.

Half an hour later I was in position at via Don Bosco. Raffaello Beggiato arrived a couple minutes early. I let him stand there, smoking, till the stroke of midnight.

"Motherfucker, here goes Contin," he blurted when he saw me.

"That's right. Siviero won't be coming."

"Who's Siviero?"

I burst out laughing. "Honor among thieves right to the end, eh?"

He looked around. "I expected to see the cops show up. Ten minutes ago I shook off a couple that were tailing me. But you're a real surprise."

"No police. Just you and me."

"How'd you find out about Siviero?"

"You'll never know."

"Where is he now?"

"I assume he took off with your cash."

He shook his head. "It can't be. You got him locked up?"

"No."

"What are you doing here?"

"I've come to tell you your dream of running away has gone up in smoke. You're fucked, Beggiato. I hope the cancer kills you real slow."

I turned and went back to the car. If the murderer of Enrico and Clara knew his dollars and passport were in the trunk, he would've jumped me to get his hands on them. Instead he did nothing but stare at my back. I felt his hate. And I was happy about it.

RAFFAELLO

His mother must've been a fucking whore to give birth to a shit like him. He fucked me like I was wet behind the ears. The letter to the newspapers was just a move in his plan. He wanted to get off on telling me in person he figured out everything. Must've just happened 'cause when he came to the prison he wasn't wise to it. I don't know how he found my partner and I can't imagine what's happened to him. If the bulls grabbed him they would've already picked me up for questioning. And what about the ones tailing me? I don't understand a fucking thing anymore. All I know is I got to say goodbye to my dreams of freedom. I feel like crying but I'm too fucking pissed off. What do I do now? Start chemo and wait for the surveillance judge to find out his wife's cheating on him so he can throw me back in jail for spite? Motherfucker, I was spitting distance away from real freedom and out pops Contin to make faces at me like some snotnosed kid. You see how satisfied he was? If he had any balls he would've busted me in the chops. But he's weird, He likes playing his little games. I got to be jinxed. Fifteen years of suffering for nothing. Now I've got two cocks up my asshole. Contin and the cancer. We'll see which one hurts more.

If I start putting two and two together it always comes out my mamma. Only she could've told Contin about Siviero. The times, the details, they all fit. She must've made some kind of deal with that fucking Contin: the name in exchange for the letter to the newspapers. Now what do I do? I can't get angry at her. I got to act like nothing happened. But how do I handle that son-of-a-whore shit? Do I kill him? Cut him to shreds?

Rip out his heart and take a bite out of it? He deserves to die like a dog. If cancer was contagious I'd infect him. But I killed his wife and kid. I can't touch him. He's only getting revenge. I'd do the same. But like a man. With a gun or a knife. He's too cruel. A coward. It's too easy to get riled at me. I really want to know what happened to Oreste. But I can't just go to his house. Might run into the cops and find it was all a maneuver to get me out in the open. I can only wait now. Don't even have the cash to get wasted. I already shot all the scag I copped today. I'll head back to mamma's house and have a good cry. I feel I need it. Yeah, I want to cry. Till I'm done in. Tomorrow I'll go see Don Silvio to get some cash out of him. I don't want to be reduced to snatching bags for cigarette money. I don't want to commit any more crimes. I want to die peacefully. The time for playing cops and robbers is over.

The next day I went back to work. I paid Gastone Vallaresso for the days he took my place, and I went back behind the counter. Gastone had done a good job, nobody complained, and he always remembered to give a receipt. I was happy to get back to replacing heels and duplicating keys. I felt better, even if I couldn't think clearly about what happened at Siviero's house. The muscles in my arms and back hurt me; that was the only real sensation I felt. Everything else was obscured by the darkness of death. Even blood had a strange color, as if I were seeing it in black and white. Clara had guided my justice. And this was enough. I felt a touch of excitement when I thought about Ivana Stella. I still wasn't finished with her. In the afternoon she came by to see me at the supermarket.

"Ciao, good-looking."

"Ciao, lovely. What are you doing in these parts?"

"I wanted to see you."

"You can come see me tonight."

She blushed. "I almost never go out after a certain hour. I wouldn't know how to explain it to Vera."

She still hadn't said a word about our relationship to her daughter. I decided to have a little fun. "You're right. Then I'll come to your house."

Another blush. "She might get wind of something between us."

"You're old enough to live your life as you think best."

"Everything in its time. Don't rush it, please. I want to avoid problems with Vera."

I gave her an understanding smile. "Then we could see each other Sunday afternoon."

Before heading back home, I drove past the cleaners, Siviero's house, and the dump. The gate was down, the shutters were closed, and silence reigned amid the trash.

For dinner I defrosted a pre-cooked portion of zuppa di pesce. I added a drop of oil and stuck it in the microwave. As I ate, I followed the news on a few local channels. No one had yet noticed Oreste and Daniela's disappearance.

It was only a question of days, and then it would become a juicy news item for journalists and bar gossips. I wasn't worried. In fact, I felt a bit curious. For the first time since the tragedy, the future actually seemed interesting to me.

The first articles appeared on Sunday. As I left the cemetery, I noticed the headlines at the newsstand: "Couple Missing. Relatives Suspect Foul Play." I bought the three dailies. They reported substantially the same information, leaked by the police and the command of the carabinieri. Daniela Borsatto's parents and Oreste Siviero's sister, worried they hadn't heard from either, learned that the cleaners had been closed for several days, and they received no answer when they knocked on the door of the house on via San Domenico. They then reported the disappearance to the police. Investigators were proceeding with caution, given the nature of the case. The couple were adults and could have decided to go on vacation for a few days. They made clear, all the same, that the routine procedures had been set in motion. They questioned neighbors in the vicinity and customers at the cleaners. Everyone expressed surprise. They described the couple as punctual, methodical, and friendly. I threw the papers in a trash can and went back home. I had to do some cleaning before Ivana Stella arrived.

Sexually, the woman was a disaster. All she knew how to do

was keep her legs open and pant with a certain degree of participation. I cruelly forced her to confront the issue.

"It's all my husband's fault," she squawked at one point.

"Maybe this is why he left you. A little imagination never hurts in bed."

"Could we change the subject?" She was in a huff.

"I like you a lot, Ivana Stella, but I'm looking for a complete woman. Maybe we should just drop everything."

"Please, don't talk that way. You'll see, I'll learn. I'll be good, I promise you."

I gave her a couple pats on the bottom. "Then next time we'll start here."

On Monday the local channels broadcast the news about the discovery of Siviero's SUV.

On Tuesday the police forced open the gate at the cleaners and the door of the house. Absolutely no trace of the Siviero couple.

Two days later, while I was making a copy of a butterfly key, Superintendent Valiani came by. He lit a cigarette and waited for me to finish the job.

"I'm surprised to see you here," I said calmly.

The cop pulled an envelope out of his jacket pocket and showed me a color photo. The subject was me. I was strolling on the sidewalk near the cleaners.

"I don't understand," I stammered.

"There are others. The narcs were keeping an eye on the African hairdresser's next to Siviero's shop; bosses in the Nigerian mafia used to get together there. You were spotted in the area many times. But you were interested in the cleaners, and you certainly weren't a regular customer. We found one receipt made out in your name."

"So what?"

"I've been a cop too long not to find the coincidence a bit strange. What was your relationship to Oreste Siviero and Daniela Borsatto?"

"I was their customer. That's it."

"I combed through the archive and discovered Siviero had been a suspect in a number of robberies. He always got off because we never managed to find enough evidence. Earlier he did a stretch in prison for car theft."

"Why are you telling me all this?"

"Because Siviero used to hang out at a pool hall where Raffaello Beggiato was often seen."

"Do you think he's the accomplice?"

"I don't think anything. I'm only trying to understand. Something isn't right here."

He threw his butt on the floor and left without saying goodbye. I went back to work. I wasn't worried. I had a clean conscience.

RAFFAELLO

When the bulls came to pick me up I nearly shit myself. For a moment I was convinced they were taking me back to prison. But that fuckface Valiani only wanted to question me. Right away he made it clear they had something on me, they saw me buying drugs from the Albanians, but they didn't give a fuck about this. He wanted to know why I'd snuck out of the house eleven o'clock one night and shaken off his men. Who did I meet? Nobody, superintendent, I got cancer, you really don't think I'm going to start fucking up now, do you? Then he asked me if I knew Oreste Siviero. Who? That guy that disappeared with his wife? No, never seen him. Fifteen years ago I used to go to the same bar? After all this time you expect me to remember? At that point he started hitting me with questions about Contin. He wanted to know what we said during the talk in prison. Nothing in particular, superintendent, the usual bullshit. He wanted to make sure I was sorry. I tried to convince him but he'd already made up his mind. And I understand why. If I was in his shoes I wouldn't be in no forgiving mood either. He also asked me if Siviero and Contin knew each other. I didn't think, just asked "Why?" He didn't answer. He made the usual cop threats and threw me out of his office. The problem is I don't know what to think. Oreste disappeared and left me hanging. Contin comes into it in a big way but I can't figure out how. And I can't even go around looking for him. The bulls got their eye on me and I ain't got the cash to take off. Don Silvio gave me a hundred euros: what the fuck am I supposed to do with this chump change? I went to the hospital to take tests and it's worse there than in jail. The doctors and nurses are a bunch of shitheads. They treat me bad, look down on me. Give me nasty sticks with those needles. When they're together they call me "the lifer" out loud and I'm ashamed. I can't think about dying surrounded by all this hate. To tell the truth, I don't really want to die but these people won't lift a finger to save me. No, they'll make me suffer. The motherfucking torturers. What do I do now? I'm trapped like a rat. And I've been this way ever since I killed two innocent people. But I don't deserve it. Fuck, I got cancer. But does anybody here got any pity?

SILVANO

I went to the bar in the supermarket to get a coffee. Valiani was sitting at a table with Gastone Vallaresso. They were too busy talking to spot me. It wasn't hard to imagine the topic of that conversation. The superintendent was reconstructing my movements. I hadn't gone to work on the days the Siviero couple disappeared, and that fact had to make him think twice. Let him rack his brain. The trash was piled high, layer after layer. They'd never be found. The most annoying thing was that they were wasting time with me while criminals roamed the city streets undisturbed. Valiani was past it. He was just a stupid old man who squandered the taxpayers' money while he waited to start collecting his pension. I expected him to come and ask me more questions, but he walked by Heels in a Jiffy without even deigning me a glance.

He came back the next day. "Signor Contin, you never cease to surprise me," he said, a false smile printed on his face.

"And why is that?"

"You've been a widower for many years. And like many single men you go with prostitutes. But I never would've imagined you'd become a regular customer of Giorgia Valente."

"She's a sex professional, like so many others."

"Not really. She was Raffaello Beggiato's woman, and that makes her special."

"May I know why you're looking into my private life?"

"Can't you guess?"

"No."

"Let's sum up the facts. On a number of occasions you were seen in front of the Sivieros' cleaners for reasons that aren't clear. You seemed to be checking up on them. And during this same period you had someone replace you at work, something you never did before. Then on the day before the couple's disappearance—this is truly out of the ordinary, if you'll allow me to put it that way—you drive sixty kilometers to go to another supermarket, where you buy a spade, a pickaxe, six plastic sheets, and three rolls of packing tape for a total of thirty-seven euros and forty cents. Your debit card payment shows all this."

"I see you've been keeping busy."

"What did you do with all that stuff?"

"It's none of your business."

"Bad answer. But the surprises don't stop here. Someone who resembles you, driving an automobile identical to yours, was seen in the vicinity of the Sivieros' house. Inside the house forensics came across some prints that don't belong to the owners. They aren't yours, are they?"

"Where are you heading?"

"I'm convinced you're somehow involved in the Sivieros' disappearance, and when I think about the spade and the pickaxe, I get some unpleasant hunches."

"You're letting your imagination run away with you."

"Listen, Signor Contin, I'm not against you. And in fact I still haven't said anything to the judge, not even to my colleagues. I'm only trying to understand how you got yourself mixed up in this mess."

"There's nothing to understand. Focus on your other cases. I imagine there's plenty of work at the station."

He shook his head, disappointed, and walked away, blending into the crowd of customers. I was sure he'd come back. That's the way cops work.

When I got home, I took the suitcase from the car and hid it in a neighbor's storage space. The widow Mandruzzato was almost ninety, and she hadn't left her apartment for a while. A Romanian housekeeper took care of her, paid by her children, but they rarely came by. It was a safe place. Not even Valiani would think of sticking his nose in there. Besides, only I and Beggiato knew the money and passport existed.

The following morning I noticed the superintendent sitting in a car parked in front of my building. He did nothing to prevent himself from being noticed. He followed me to the supermarket. In the middle of the morning I went to get my usual coffee. I thought I saw Valiani in the housewares section. On my way back to the shop, I suddenly turned and spotted him putting a cup, a spoon, and a saucer in a plastic bag. I smiled in admiration. I really didn't expect this move. I'd see the cop again soon enough. He'd ask me why my prints were in Siviero's house.

A famous program that dealt with missing persons devoted a long and useless show to the case. Lots of questions and hypotheses but no answers. The couple had vanished into thin air. The hosts assured the viewing audience they would continue the investigation. I switched off the TV and went to bed. I dreamt of Clara. Once we spent a weekend in London. We left Enrico with his grandparents. The first night in the hotel, Clara came out of the bathroom wearing a sheer nightgown. "I want to make love all night long," she said, slipping her hand beneath the covers. I woke up crying.

I found Valiani waiting for me, leaning against my car. As usual, he was smoking. I'd given it up when I started to deal in wines. Smoke ruins the palate.

"I noticed you haven't read the papers in a few days."

"Maybe I don't want to."

"Or maybe you know more than the journalists do."

I snorted. Valiani's attitude was irritating. "What do you want now?"

"The prints found in the house are yours, Signor Contin. They're in the kitchen, the living room, the bedroom, and the bathroom. Forensics also found dark stains on the ceiling of one room. The rest of it was clean, but there were traces of adhesive on the walls, as if someone had attached some sheets with packing tape. Now the hematologists are analyzing the stains. They could be blood. If that were the case, they would analyze the DNA to see if it belongs to the Sivieros."

"I don't follow."

"I think you do. And I'm equally certain you're not over-joyed to learn you made a mistake."

"What would that be?"

"The blood on the ceiling."

"If it is blood."

"I'd bet on it. It would show, in any case, that Oreste and Daniela were killed in that room. The likely m.o. was a blunt object or a blade moved up and down to strike the victims. Numerous times and with considerable violence. When the weapon was lifted upward, rising above the murderer's head, blood spattered the ceiling."

"Interesting theory."

"Which will soon become an established fact in the investigation. The classic wedge, as we old cops call it. A few loose ends remain before we can close the case. For example, on the day of their disappearance, the Sivieros behaved strangely. Daniela didn't show up at the cleaners that morning, and Oreste closed the shop at 12:30. Neither of them was seen again. However, you, Signor Contin, judging from the story told by your debit card, bought two bottles of wine and a bottle of cognac after 14:00. Do you recall what you did before and after? Especially after."

"I spent the afternoon at home."

"By yourself, I imagine."

"You're mistaken. I was with a lady."

"And does this lady have a name?"

"Of course. Ivana Stella Tessitore."

The superintendent showed signs of weakening. His theory

was now on shaky ground. But he wasn't the kind of guy who'd throw in the towel just yet. "Until what time did you entertain this woman?"

"I don't remember. Ask her."

"I won't fail to. I'd like to tell you a secret, Signor Contin. I haven't told anyone the prints in the Siviero house are yours."

"You're concealing a lot of information that concerns me. Why ever would you do that?"

"It would set going the judicial process. You would receive formal notification that you're a suspect in a criminal investigation, and in all probabilty you'd wind up in the Court of Assizes. But the trial would be based on circumstantial evidence, and you'd be acquitted. We in turn would be eating humble pie because you've been the victim of a horrible crime. The newspapers would crucify us. And then again I'm not so sure I want to see you in prison. There might be another way to resolve the matter."

"Is that so?"

"You worry me. You act like this thing doesn't have anything to do with you. Are you sure you're feeling O.K.?"

"Are you asking me if I suffer from a psychological disorder? I'm glad somebody is raising this issue—after fifteen years."

RAFFAELLO

I had to give mamma hell. "Please tell me the truth about what you did," I told her. "No matter how bad it is, I won't get angry. You're the most important person in my life and I'll always love you." That made her talk. The fucking bitch, she cooked up a real mess and thought she was helping me. To comfort her I had to shower her with kisses. Fact is, without Contin's letter to the papers I would've never made it out. But then I got fucked. Still, I can think through this thing clearly now. Oreste put together the money and the passport for my getaway. Contin learned about it and blackmailed him, or made him take off, or whacked him with his wife. There are no other possibilites. But do you really see a normal guy like Contin killing two fucking people? He ain't like me, that guy. If I hadn't been wired on coke that day I would've never pulled the trigger. The real problem is finding out what's happened to my cash. If Oreste hit the road he took it with him. But in that case he should be contacting me soon to give me at least part of it. He knows I've got no time to lose. If Contin took it, he still hasn't handed it over to the bulls. This much I'm sure about. But the thing I really don't understand is why Contin didn't run to Valiani to tell him about Oreste. He must've been planning all along to get revenge. Then Contin the execution-er killed them. But Oreste's quick and no push-over. I don't see how he could've let himself be fucked by somebody like Contin. I'll wait a couple days and if my partner doesn't turn up I'll go have a chat with the inconsolable widower. He's got to give me the money. No matter what. I'll blackmail him. I swore to mamma I wouldn't commit any more crimes. And I swore to myself. But there's no other way out of this. Contin's doing just fine. He must have a nice little pile stashed away in the bank. We're in the northeast, after all. Here every honest citizen's got his shitty bank account. And if he don't shell out I'll squeal to Valiani. Fuck, for fifteen years my lips were sealed and now I'm ready to sell out anyfuckingbody. But I'll just be bluffing. I couldn't be a rat.

SILVANO

I was trying to digest the meatballs in tomato sauce from the rosticceria, watching a special edition of my favorite quiz show, when someone rang the doorbell. I got up reluctantly to answer it. That night, instead of the usual contestants, they had celebrities. They couldn't answer most of the questions, but they were clever and amusing, turning their ignorance into entertainment. When I saw it was Ivana Stella, I was less annoyed by the interruption. It could turn out to be an interesting night.

"Why on earth did you come at this hour?" I asked. "Did your daughter let you out?"

Signora Tessitore was in no mood for jokes. "I've just come from the police station, not from home. A superintendent called Valiani sent for me. He wanted to know if I'd spent a certain afternoon here in your company. How could you humiliate me like this?"

I offered her a healthy shot of cognac. "I needed an alibi. That cop suspects I'm implicated in the disappearance of the Siviero couple."

"That's clear. He asked me if I knew them or heard you talk about them. You mustn't allow me to get mixed up in this. How embarrassing! I had to admit we've had sexual relations."

"You told the truth. Don't blow this out of proportion. Nothing serious happened."

"For you perhaps. I had to answer very intimate questions."

"Like what?"

"Valiani asked how and when we met, and he wanted to know if it was the first time I came here. And especially if it was you who asked me to come."

The superintendent was shrewd. He suspected I was using Ivana Stella as an alibi. "Did he ask you anything else?"

"Why? Doesn't this seem like enough to you?"

"You're overreacting for someone who makes a habit of visiting prison convicts. You should know by now how that world works."

"I don't like your tone. Instead of apologizing for involving me in an embarrassing situation, you mock me because of my volunteer work."

"What work? You're just a frustrated woman who devotes herself to good deeds to give meaning to your life because your marriage failed."

"I won't allow you to insult me."

"Shut up. You're not capable of holding on to a husband because you don't know how to satisfy a man. And now the inmates aren't enough for you anymore. You've started to drink."

"You're cruel. I thought you loved me."

"Strip and you'll see how I love you."

She snatched her bag and headed for the door. "I'm leaving."

"Go out that door, and for sure you'll never see me again."

She hesitated for a moment. "I'll stay only if you change your attitude."

"Of course. Right now I just want to have sex."

"I don't."

"Then there's the door."

"Please, don't treat me like this."

"Don't you waste my time."

She sat back down on the couch and poured herself another cognac. "Let's talk, Silvano."

"Later. Now get undressed."

"No. I want to know what you have to do with the disappearance of the Siviero couple."

"That's nothing that concerns you."

"Can I know why you're so hostile towards me?"

I jumped up and grabbed the dictionary. I leafed through it till I found what I wanted. "A sentence," I started to read out loud, "is a punitive measure provided by a judicial system for transgressions against the law, commensurate with their gravity. Synonyms: chastisement, punishment, sanction, penalty.

"Do you understand? Prison is a place of expiation where rules are in force, and inmates have rights and duties. Nowhere is it written that a sentence provides for consolation. Only those who've suffered from the actions of criminals are entitled to that."

I was shouting and shaking with rage. Ivana Stella stared at me, frightened. I took the photos of Enrico and Clara from the drawer and shoved them under her nose. "Look at their open chests, empty, black. When the autopsy was finished, the organs were thrown back inside any old way, and the bodies were sewn up slapdash with thick nylon thread. No one has ever consoled me for this. The words of comfort have never gone beyond the obvious. That's what insults you and gnaws at your mind till you're driven mad with pain. And rage."

I was out of breath. Ivana Stella had turned pale. "Calm down, Silvano, I understand—"

"No, you don't understand," I interrupted her. "Otherwise you'd side with the victims, not the convicts."

"Prison makes people worse than they are," she said calmly. "We try to help inmates understand their mistakes so once they're out they won't commit more crimes. That's all."

"And us?"

"You victims receive justice at the trial. This is why the law exists. The state can't help you overcome the pain, but people can. And I wanted to be with you for this reason as well. But especially because I'd fallen in love with you. You seemed a special person to me, but you're just wrong and desperate."

She stood up and took her bag. "You used me, took advantage of me. I only hope you've had nothing to do with those missing people."

"Maybe I'll become one of your beneficiaries."

She sighed. She looked older and tired. "Get some help, Silvano. There might still be time."

I was disappointed. I didn't manage to punish Ivana Stella, just make her suffer. She stood up to me, but I made myself sound ridiculous with those vulgarities about sex. Rage drove me to bare my soul and show her the autopsy photos. I shouldn't have done that. It was disrespectful to Clara and Enrico.

I pulled out the bottle of Vecchia Romagna. Slipped on the headphones and started to listen to The Pooh. Clara had liked their songs so much. My woman, my love, the mother of my son. I tried to resist the alcohol, but at a certain point it laid me out like I'd been socked in the jaw.

I woke up in the morning with my face dirty from dried vomit. Before I got into the shower, I cleaned the floor.

When I opened Heels in a Jiffy, Valiani was already there waiting for me. He wanted to get on my nerves, but I wasn't one of his ex-cons.

"Something dawned on me," he said, searching for the lighter in his pocket. "I think Oreste Siviero had put together his partner's share of the loot. You know why? I went back and reread the transcript of his interrogation fifteen years ago. Beggiato always said he couldn't give up his accomplice's name because the guy was saving his cash. It was safer than if he'd put it in a bank because Siviero could never screw him. Beggiato would get mad and rat him out."

"Your theories are always fascinating, superintendent. But what can a miserable cancer victim do with all that money if he's doomed to die in a couple years?"

"It's one thing to die poor, another to die rolling in cash.

Besides, you need to be familiar with the jailbird mindset. Beggiato hung on to his dream of the money for fifteen long years. To have it at his disposal even for a little while would make him feel better."

"You talk about it as if you're sure the money exists."

"It's a conviction based on indisputable evidence, my dear Contin. While examining the phone records for the cleaners, I found a number in Canton Ticino belonging to a known fence who also has a sideline: he changes money for the underworld."

"Changes money?"

"Suppose you need euros changed fast. He takes ten percent and gives you dollars in return. Or other currencies. But in this case they were dollars. My colleagues in Lugano have confirmed it."

"And I bet you've also kept this detail quiet."

"You guessed right. I'm certain those lovely greenbacks are now in your hands. And I'm thinking how they might make a nice supplement to my pension."

"Am I mistaken or are you offering me a deal?"

"The best deal of your life. My silence in exchange for the money."

"Otherwise you'll arrest me?"

"The judge would certainly find the evidentiary support sufficient for an arrest warrant. Blood and fingerprints are nasty business."

"I doubt a Court of Assizes would be convinced. You don't have the bodies. Maybe there was no murder. Siviero might have staged this charade to make off with Beggiato's money."

"Among the blood stains on the ceiling forensics also found microtraces of brain matter. There can be no doubt we're dealing with a double homicide. At this point, we're looking for two corpses. You'll read about it in the papers tomorrow."

"And when would Siviero and his wife have been killed?"

"The same day as their disappearance."

"But I have an alibi."

"You entertained Signora Tessitore in the afternoon. You could have murdered them after or just before. We would need the corpses to determine the time of death. I do agree, in any case, that what you call an alibi could seriously jeopardize the charge."

"I think so too. An honest citizen doesn't philander with a lady on the same day he commits a premeditated double homicide."

"The rest of the evidence is so strong that the case would nonetheless go to trial."

"I don't think so. I am Silvano Contin, the man whose wife and son were killed."

"Do you really think this makes you untouchable? It's in your interest to consider my proposal carefully. It's your only way out."

I stood watching him as he walked away, dragging his feet. His left heel was worn down more than the right one. Typical of someone who suffers from sciatica. Shoes tell you a lot about the person who wears them. Their standard of living, first of all, and their social position. Valiani's were a pair of black moccasins with laces. He couldn't have paid more than forty euros for them. He was right: a little money would come in handy for him.

I'd been on the outside a few days already and I still hadn't gotten laid. What a joke. I never thought this would happen to me all those times I jerked off in my cell. I saw so much cunt on the street, my cock was hard for a good part of the day. I needed a woman. On the double. I was afraid the chemo would shrivel up my cock. Seeing as how I had no cash, or at least I didn't have much, I went to Giorgia Valente. To her house, not where she worked. The most she'd do was tell me to go to hell. When she opened the door my jaw dropped. Fuck, she really changed. The babe of fifteen years ago had turned into a fat ugly broad. Life didn't deal her a good hand. The oldest profession in the world is also the hardest. If you're not lucky enough to find a fool to marry you, or not sharp enough to manage the capital between your legs, you wind up giving it away as long as you can and then you've got nothing left. No pension to enjoy and least of all the thought that you had a reason to live. I've known so many desperate old whores. Giorgia was doomed to become just like them.

"You're always beautiful," I mumbled to be kind and she hugged me and kissed me on the cheeks. "It's not true," she said. "You've always been such a big liar, but I'm happy to see you." She offered me a whiskey and told me about Silvano Contin right away. According to her, he's crazy and dangerous. And she knows men well. Well, fuck Contin too, crazy or sane, he's going to give me the money anyway. She changed the subject, asked me if I'd already been with a woman. I shook my head. "Then I'll take care of that," she said. I just stood there because I didn't know how to tell her I couldn't pay her. She gave me a smile and whispered not to worry. She took me to bed and gave me the works: mouth, cunt, ass. She acted as if she was my woman. A real sweetie. She whispered words of love in my ear and I was happy. Great woman, Giorgia Valente. She knew I needed a woman's warmth, especially, not just a good fuck. In the end, I fell asleep in her arms and when I opened my eyes again she smiled at me. A real smile. At that point, I felt like crying. It'd been fifteen years since something like that happened. She comforted me. "Sleep with me tonight," she said and got up to make dinner. We also watched TV like a real couple. The next morning she brought me coffee in bed and we made love again. When I left to go to the hospital I felt lightheaded; jail and death seemed so far away. I was sure the day would turn out good but the hospital was a bummer. As soon as I got there they told me the first chemo session would happen the next day. One nurse looked real pleased when she said I'd lose my hair. So did another one when she said I'd throw up my guts. Then she added I didn't have any guts. The fucking cunts. They were young and pretty. I should just put up with it and not say anything. I would've gladly kicked their asses but they'd get revenge later. Fuck, I'm afraid of chemo. I don't ever expect to see Oreste again and I really need Contin's money to get shitfaced. So I'm not aware I'm dying and if I see myself bald in the mirror I'll only feel like laughing. When I went back home Valiani was there. That asshole packed me in his car and made me take a spin. He asked me another bunch of questions about Contin. "I don't know nothing. How else can I put it?" But he kept on bringing up my share of the loot. He wanted to know where and when I was supposed to meet Siviero. I just kept stonewalling. In the heat of the moment he came out with the name of our trusted fence. I knew for sure then. Oreste was all ready to hand over my share. The bull was talking but I wasn't listening. I was thinking about skipping chemo the following day. I didn't want to throw up on Contin when I asked him for the dough.

"I brought you the newspaper," said Valiani as he opened it on the counter of my shop.

I set my eyes on the full-page headline: "Daniela Borsatto and Oreste Siviero Murdered at Home. Investigators Call It a Brutal, Premeditated Crime. Motive Remains a Mystery. Police Scour City and Province in Search of the Bodies."

"Have you thought about my proposal?" asked the superintendent.

I limited myself to a shrug. Each and every word might prove to be risky.

"At this point, I have to speed things up and deliver a report to the judge," the cop continued. "Today's Thursday. I'll come by again Monday morning. It'll be your last chance. Either the money or jail."

I didn't have the vaguest idea what I should do. I felt like I was being sucked into the vortex of events, sinking even deeper into the darkness that engulfed my mind. Maybe paying for Valiani's silence was the best way to avoid problems and put behind me the incident concerning Siviero and his wife. But I wasn't keen on the idea. Learning the superintendent was corrupt had been a nasty blow, difficult to accept. For too long I'd placed my trust in the wrong cop.

Thinking only confused me, and I started to feel slightly dazed. Maybe I was still hung over from the night before. I started to work, and right away I felt better. A heel, a sole, a key. Nails, hammer, brush, cutter. My hands moved confidently, and I observed them with satisfaction.

That night I closed a little early and went shopping. I noticed the superintendent watching me from a distance. I was tempted to go up to him and say I decided to accept his proposal and hand over the money. But thinking had become even more of an effort, and I let it go. I was also picking out the würstel at that moment, and I didn't want to make the same mistake of buying the chicken ones. I piled a good supply of frozen food in the cart and headed for the check out.

"You're single," said the cashier as she passed the things over the optical reader. "The pre-cooked dishes give you away."

"Yeah, that's right. When you're alone, you don't have much desire to cook."

"Separated?"

"Widower."

"I'm sorry, I didn't mean—"

"Don't worry."

"You know, I just got the urge to talk to you because I've started eating the same things too."

"Then you're lucky. Until a few years ago this stuff was really crap."

The cashier looked at me in a strange way. She hadn't understood the meaning of my words. And yet she was in fact lucky. Nowadays supermarkets are full of food geared for people who live alone, but these products used to be rare and bad-quality. I now have fifteen years' experience, and I vividly remember the ravioli packaged with a ragù so acidic it gave you cramps. Or the first trays of frozen cannelloni and lasagna, where the pasta seemed to be chipped and you needed an entire day to digest it. Evidently single people had become a viable market and as such were worthy of attention. I continued to think about the evolution of pre-cooked meals till I got home. A good sign. My mind was slowly beginning to function again. Every so often the faces of Oreste and Daniela would peek out of the darkness, provoking anxiety, but they disappeared almost immediately.

I was surprised but not frightened when I found Beggiato sitting calmly on the couch. From the expression on his face I knew right away his intentions weren't bad. On his knees lay the same daily Valiani brought me.

"How did you get inside?"

He showed me a jimmy. "Your lock's worth shit. I advise you to change it before some Gypsies clean out your apartment."

I placed the bags on the kitchen table. "What do you want?"

"How does it feel to become a murderer?"

"You tell me."

"I understand about killing Oreste, but what the fuck did the woman have to do with it?"

The words popped right out of me. "She was his accomplice. She took his side. She let herself be fucked in the ass just to save him."

"Maybe she loved him, and that's all there was to it."

"They were animals. Like you."

"Why did you do it?"

"Justice."

"Ah, you're a fucking executioner like Charles Bronson."

"I exercised my right."

"Do you realize you're a murderer?"

"You're the murderer. I was the hangman."

"You're crazy, and I'm a dickhead. It's all my fault."

"What are you saying?"

"I was the one that shot your kid and your wife. You killed Oreste for nothing."

"But you always pointed the finger at him."

"That's different. I was blaming a ghost to avoid a life sentence."

"You were still accomplices. The punishment is the same, as the code stipulates."

The murderer grinned in my face. "You want to kill me too?"

"No. The cancer will take care of you. And it'll be worse.

You'll have time to see the darkness. Like my Clara. 'Everything's gone dark,' she said before she died. 'I'm scared.'"

"Chill out. You've got me spooked."

"I don't feel sorry for you."

Beggiato clenched his fists, but then calmed down. "How did you kill them?"

"I beat them."

"Like dogs."

"Exactly. Like dogs."

"What did you do with the bodies?"

"I buried them in the dump near the overpass."

Beggiato remained silent a couple minutes. "I just can't imagine how a 'normal' guy like you could've organized such a careful plan."

"Clara guided me."

"Clara?"

"Yes, my wife."

He jumped to his feet. "You're really out of your gourd! You're like one of those crazy fuckers I was in jail with, the ones that have 'diminished mental capacity.'"

"Stop talking bullshit and tell me what you want."

"The money."

"It's already Valiani's."

"What the fuck does that cop have to do with it?"

"He figured out everything. Or almost. He's blackmailing me. He wants the money by Monday, otherwise he'll spill everything to the judge."

Beggiato burst out laughing. "Apart from being crazy, you're a fucking dope. The superintendent isn't dirty; that bastard has never been on the take in his life. He's drawing you into a trap to get some proof positive."

"Maybe you're right. But you're not going to get the money."

"I'll go straight to the judge and report everything you told me."

"Suit yourself. It's your word against mine, lifer."

Beggiato lit a cigarette. Then he poured himself a glass of Vecchia Romagna. "I could never turn you in. I'm no rat," he said, resigned. "All the same, you're fucked. Executioner my ass. How do you think you're going to get away with it? Valiani's got you cornered."

"It's none of your business."

"I don't think you'll enjoy my death much from a prison cell. You really don't have a clue about what's waiting for you."

"No judge will have the courage to convict me."

"Wake up, bud. They convict innocent people. It's in your interest to find a good lawyer. Maybe with a psychiatrist's report you can get off with twelve, fourteen years," he said as he headed for the door. "Addio, asshole" was his goodbye.

I tossed the glass the murderer had used into the trash can, removed the cover from the couch where he sat, and stuffed it in the washer. Then I stretched out on the bed to think. The guilty weren't the problem anymore. Now I had to confront the law. If Valiani wasn't a dirty cop, as Beggiato claimed, then it meant he had no other evidence than what he'd stubbornly listed in the course of our meetings. It might be enough to drag me into the Court of Assizes or even to get me thrown into jail. Guided by Clara, I tried hard to organize a perfect plan precisely to avoid creating problems with the investigators. But I'd made a series of errors that didn't escape Valiani. I reviewed the facts and hypotheses. In the end, I decided to trust Beggiato's judgment and not give the money to the superintendent. I also decided that under no circumstances would I defend myself. The charge would've been so unjust as not to merit any consideration. I wouldn't respond to any questions from the judges or the police. Silence would be my weapon to prevent the court from any possible confusion of justice with homicide. I felt peaceful and fell asleep. I dreamt that Clara was taking Enrico for a bike ride. They were smiling. They passed by without seeing me.

RAFFAELLO

Today's Monday. Another shitty fucking day. Even free. I got to cross the street but can't make up my mind. I'll smoke another cigarette and then go. I decided to end this business once and for all. What a fucking mess. It's all my fault. I've always put my foot in it. Always slipped up. Had fifteen years to think and my head's full of shit. Contin's gone off his rocker. Giorgia's right: he's a dangerous lunatic. When I left his place my blood ran cold. I felt like I was dead. That asshole calmly confessed he killed Oreste and his woman, "guided" by the wife Clara. 'Cept she's dead and buried. I remember only too well when I shot her in the belly. He beat them to death. What a monster. That's what he's become. This business has got to be stopped forever. Four dead because of a fucking robbery—that's too many. I'll finish this cigarette, slip in that entrance and say the last word. Stop, that's it. Up to me to do it. I'm the only one that can stop this business from going on forever. After the meeting with that freaky-deak Contin I started to think. Crossed the whole town trying to get my brain working, at least once. And finally everything was clear. I went to Giorgia's. Told her I wanted to go to the sea. She understood. Whores got the gift of mind-reading. In the morning she got dressed up like a lady and picked me up in her car. We went to the Romagna coast. A place that's packed with hotels. Nearly all of them empty this time of year. We got a room in a pretty little joint. Elegant and discreet. I wanted to go to the beach right away but Giorgia said she wanted to make love first. That's how she put it. Not screw, fuck, or get dicked. Make love. She desired me. I felt like crying again and she licked the tears from my face. Then she got on top of me and slowly moved that big ass of hers, whispering sweet words that made me feel good. We took a long walk by the sea, didn't say a word, just held hands. Every once in a while I stopped and looked in the distance, filling my eyes with life and freedom, and then she gave me a big hug. As usual I was flat broke but Giorgia thought of everything. In the afternoon she took me to a boutique and dressed me from head to toe. For dinner we went to a top-drawer restaurant. Some TV star was there, eating with a dynamite chick. We drank champagne. Lots of it. I cased the joint and saw only wealth and people having a blast. I had cancer, working to do me in even then, plus four corpses and that fucking nut Contin all spinning around my brain and none of it seemed real anymore. At times I told myself I was just like everybody else. Giorgia was running off at the mouth. But she never brought up anything ugly. She talked like a wife. I don't know if she was faking it or if like me she was taking advantage of that seaside trip to put her shitty life behind her. I just don't know. I know only that when I die I'll think of her. That night in bed I couldn't get it up. Too much champagne. That really made me feel like shit. She told me not to worry about it. She cuddled me like a baby and the next morning my dick was hard as a rock. She started giving me head when I was still asleep. What a way to wake up, kiddo! When I took a shower I felt a little sad thinking I could've had her at my side if I didn't kill that mamma and her son. Saturday night we went dancing. Ballroom dancing. I didn't remember a step, looked like a bear at the circus. We laughed so much. And drank. The next morning we went back to the beach. I took off my shoes and socks and went into the water. It was freezing. But I didn't feel a thing. In front of me stood only sea and sky. I started to walk out till Giorgia grabbed me by the shoulders. "Where are you going, amore?" she asked and just then I realized the water had reached my waist.

That's when I told her what I decided to do. "Why?" she asked me.

"It's hard to explain. I told you only so you won't think bad of me."

We went back to town in the dead of night and I was wasted with sadness. She wanted me to stay and sleep at her place but I had to say goodbye to mamma. Giorgia started crying, kissed me on the forehead, and went back to being a whore. Today's Monday. Another shitty fucking day. The cigarette's done and I got to make a decision. Before leaving I hugged mamma. She cried too. I'm really fed the fuck up now. And I'm heading across this motherfucking street.

SILVANO

I spent all Sunday morning at the cemetery. I cleaned the graves and spoke to Clara and Enrico. It was a beautiful day, and the sun crept between the stones and statues, creating strange luminous effects. On my way back home I stopped at the rosticceria and the newstand. The headlines about the Siviero case still took up a good part of the front page. Aside from the usual interviews with relatives and neighbors, there wasn't any news worth noting. A well-informed "source" had leaked the hypothesis of a double crime devised by the criminal underworld. I cleaned the house from top to bottom and towards evening packed a bag with clothes, pajamas, a toothbrush, and toothpaste. Then I went to sleep. I was very tired.

Monday morning I opened the shop as usual. I slid the bag under the counter and started to serve customers, waiting for Valiani to arrive. The superintendent didn't turn up. Not even in the afternoon. I thought he'd show later. But I waited for him all night, sitting in front of the TV. I was puzzled. I didn't know what to think. While I was shaving, I convinced myself that Valiani had understood the meaning of my actions. But I was wrong. I realized when I opened the newspaper. "Breakthrough on the Double Homicide. Suspect in Custody."

RAFFAELLO

That shitface Valiani gave me a wicked kick in the shins. "What the fuck are you making up?" he started to shout. "Nothing, superintendent. I've come to give myself up." He got even more angry. Turned red in the face and repeated Contin was the one that killed Oreste and his wife. "Why?" he kept on asking. "Why are you sacrificing yourself for him? What's the point? You realize they'll throw you back in jail and you'll croak like a dog in the clinic?" Yep, like a dog. Like Oreste and Daniela. I couldn't really explain why to him. I had to play dickhead till nightfall. The superintendent wanted to fuck over Contin but I couldn't let that happen. The whole business would've gone on forever. They'd make me go back to court and testify and I didn't want to do that. The truth was I felt sorry for Contin. I saw so many lifers go crazy from desperation and he was just like them. Sentenced to a life of pain. It was all my fault. I killed his wife and kid, I didn't have the courage to admit it so I accused my partner, and I set in motion the mechanism that led him to track down Oreste. I sure felt sorry for him but I couldn't explain it to Valiani. He wouldn't understand. He thinks like a cop. The good guys belong on the outside, the bad guys on the inside. Contin wasn't made for jail. He couldn't survive and the madness would devour him whole. Nobody takes care of the crazies in jail. Not even in the hospital for the criminally insane. Just the fact they're kept locked up drives them out of their heads even more. No. Contin shouldn't end up in a cell. Nobody would save him. Besides, he's got a right to a second chance. They always denied me that. On the outside he can get it. He can realize he's a murderer and get his shit together. Paying for him is my way of making amends for the evil I did. I couldn't tell the superintendent all this. He kept on slapping me till my face was swollen. Wanted me to retract. Finally he asked me, "How d'you kill them?"

"I beat them," was my answer.

"Where'd you bury them?"

"In the dump near the overpass."

Then he started to think. Gave me a strange look. Even he seemed nuts. "If we don't find them," he said, "it means you've made up everything. You'll get charged for it, and I'll kick your ass all the way home. But if you're telling the truth, it means you talked to Contin. Only he could've told you where he hid the bodies."

"Come off it, superintendent," I said. "Contin has nothing to do with it. It was me. Oreste wanted to take my share so I laid him out. Him and his whore."

"What kind of deal did you make? What did he promise you?" He was almost begging me to give him an answer.

They found the bodies at night, digging with a bulldozer and beaming the ground with photoelectric cells. I was there, handcuffed to a steering wheel. They also found an axe handle dirty with blood. I signed the confession and now I'm back in jail. Valiani did all he could to reason with the judge but the judge laughed in his face. The superintendent slammed his badge down on the desk and left.

I did what I had to do. I feel like shit but I don't give a fuck. It's only a question of time before the cancer fixes me forever. Before going to the police station I stopped in the cathedral. There was a sign that read "Penitents" and under it the times for confession. I knelt down and told the priest I killed a woman and a child, did a stretch in prison, and now I was going back to die there. He assured me I had God's forgiveness. Good to know. You can never be sure what you'll find when you close your eyes forever. I asked him what he knew of that business about the darkness, what Contin was telling me. The priest's answer was God is light. Up your ass, Contin. Fuck that priest too. I already told the judge I won't go to the trial. They got the confession so they can do without me. Soon they're going to transfer me to the clinic. At this point I can hardly wait. I'm writing a letter to mamma. Asking her to forgive me and not to come see me anymore. I couldn't bear her suffering. As always she got fucked over. Now she has to deal with a son that's got four deaths on his conscience. Poor mamma. Today's Tuesday. Pasta, stew, vegetable. In a little while they'll do the cell check. And then the janitor should drop by with a little dope the guys in the block gave me, something to console me for being back in jail. Let's hope it's a decent taste. So I spend the afternoon zonked and don't think about a fucking thing.

I couldn't believe Beggiato turned himself in and confessed to killing Oreste Siviero and his wife. He had no reason to do it. I read all the dailies and followed the news on the radio and the TV. It unleashed polemics and attacks against the surveillance judge. Presotto's article was distinguished by its bitter tone. The title was: "We Told You So." According to the judge responsible for the investigation, the confession was missing details, but this was to be attributed to the state of the accused's health. The bodies were discovered where Beggiato said they'd be, and that removed any doubt concerning his guilt. The motive was clear as well. Siviero had decided to hang on to his partner's share of the loot, provoking a homicidal rage. This was precisely the term used by the coroner who carried out the autopsies. He added that rarely had he seen bodies treated like that. Beggiato found himself back in prison, and he'd never leave again. Not even if the cancer spared him. The oncologist who was responsible for supervising the chemotherapy treatments ruled it out with absolute certainty. Beggiato would die in prison as I'd always wished he would.

But I was confused. Clara couldn't even help me understand why he wanted to save me. I didn't want to be beholden to him, but I couldn't deny how relieved I felt. And this made me uneasy. Nor could Valiani help me. He stopped by Heels in a Jiffy about ten days later. I was expecting his visit, even though I knew he was no longer on the force. I'd read a short notice where his early retirement was announced.

"I really can't imagine what kind of deal you made with that dumbass Beggiato."

"Unfortunately, I can't help you."

"You aren't the first guilty person I've seen get away with it. But I assure you I won't stop trying to find out why."

"The problem is you didn't want to understand from the beginning."

"Really? I'm afraid you're sick in the head, Signor Contin. You're also untouchable, sad to say. I have to admit you were right when you argued no judge would have the courage to drag you into court. Down at the police station and the prosecutor's office, everyone's ecstatic about Beggiato's confession, even though it's clear as day he's innocent."

"Everyone but you."

"In fact, when I asked if they looked for your prints on the murder weapon and the plastic sheets, they forced me to retire. The case is closed."

"I don't understand why you're so worried about animals like Beggiato and Siviero."

"The fact that Siviero is dead and Beggiato soon will be doesn't matter to me at all. I've always been in favor of capital punishment for murderers. It's just that the courts should issue the sentence and the state should execute it. This isn't the Wild West, Signor Contin, and no one has pinned a sheriff's star on your chest."

"But we victims are asked to decide whether to forgive."

Valiani stared at me with contempt. "You're not a victim anymore. You need treatment. You're sick."

The superintendent left, dragging his feet as always. I was sure I'd never see him again, and I was happy about it. At this point, no one could implicate me in that incident. The journalists had also stopped bothering me with their stupid questions about my letter of support for the suspended sentence. I'd limited myself to responding I wasn't a judge, and, besides, I'd never forgiven Beggiato.

The howl had vanished. But I didn't feel any better. I felt

even more desperate. The pain continued to throb like a festering wound. And in the darkness of my mind I now met Oreste and Daniela too. I couldn't stop thinking of Beggiato either. I was burning with curiosity to know whether he was suffering, but then sometimes I found myself hoping he wasn't. My life resumed as before. The same routines repeated over and over again in the most absolute solitude.

RAFFAELLO

What motherfucking pain! They say it's my fault 'cause I refused chemo and they're light on the morphine. The fucking torturers. I knew they'd make me suffer like hell at the clinic. I beg, implore, insult, curse. Nothing doing. I'm a multiple murderer, cruel and ruthless, and even here at the clinic these things matter. Mamma, what pain. They finally told me anyhow: I got cancer of the stomach. And now that I know I don't do nothing but hold my guts. I'm thin as a rail but at least I still got hair on my head. The only dope going around this joint is expensive and I ain't got no money to score. Besides, I can't even get out of bed. Not much time left now. The priest told me the same thing. "Be strong. Ask God to forgive your sins." "Up your fucking asshole," I shouted at him. "For more than fifteen years I been asking for forgiveness." I don't do nothing but dig up the past. And tell myself what a fucking dumbass I've been. My life was completely off track. And I'm fed up with thinking about it. Can't wait to kick and see what's on the other side. If there's a God maybe he'll take some pity on me. Contin was right about the darkness. Every so often I can't see a thing and I start shaking with fear. Who knows if that dickhead came to his senses. Let's hope he took advantage of his second chance. Shit, what a fucked-up life I had. And how fucked-up my death is. In this ward for the terminally ill there ain't nothing but death. Nobody takes any pity on you. We're the dregs of the prison system. They don't even think us worthy of croaking in a normal hospital. The sooner we're out of the way, the better. I wrote a letter to Giorgia. Kept it in the night table for almost a month. Now the time's come to send it to her.

SILVANO

Raffaello Beggiato died a few months later. I learned about it from the newspapers. I attended his funeral, although from a distance. Apart from his mother, the only people present were Giorgia Valente and Don Silvio. To one side stood the journalists, Presotto at the head of the pack. The next day his article appeared. The title was "The Solitude of the Killer."

The trial for the murders of Siviero and Borsatto was not held because of the defendant's death. The case was definitively closed. A file buried in a cabinet.

Right up to the end I hoped Beggiato would give me some sort of explanation. Every day I checked the mailbox, but nothing turned up. His death didn't leave me indifferent. Towards him I had feelings that were conflicting and always confused. Sometimes I felt as if I owed him something. Then I'd run to get the photos of Clara and Enrico out of the drawer, and the hate came back to comfort and reassure me.

The doubts proved to be a continual torment till I saw Giorgia Valente leaning on the counter of Heels in a Jiffy. She was uglier and fatter than I remembered her. I waited on the other customers, then asked how I could help her.

"You haven't come round for a while," she said. "Don't you like my ass anymore?"

"Is this what you've come to ask me?"

"No. I wanted to look you in the face. I wanted to see how someone who should be in jail right now was getting along."

"I don't understand—"

She raised a hand to interrupt me. "I know everything. Raffaello told me."

I sighed, resigned. "You want the money?"

"No. I really don't want anything from you. You make me sick. You've always made me sick."

"Then what do you want?"

"I bring you a message from Raffaello: don't waste your second chance."

"What does that mean?"

"You still don't understand?" she said, irritated. "Poor Raffaello, he died in jail to give it to you," she grumbled as she walked away.

Then she spun around and shouted. "Don't waste it, asshole. We never had it. Never!"

Everyone turned to look. Giorgia Valente stared at me hatefully. Then she walked away, clacking her heels.

EPILOGUE

Today I logged on to the internet again and visited the site of that TV program devoted to missing persons. My file is always among the "urgent" cases, despite the fact that more than a year has passed since I left my apartment one night and never returned. The newspapers pursued my case for a while. Almost everybody was convinced that I'd taken my own life because I'd left everything just as it was—the apartment, shop, car, even the garage where I kept the memories of my previous life. Good old Presotto came up with the hypothesis that I felt guilty for helping Beggiato get out of prison. Fact is, I'm alive and thriving, and I'd been thinking about taking off for a while. The death of the widow Mandruzzato forced me to retrieve the bag with the money and passport from her storage space. It stayed under my bed for a week before I decided to open it. I spread the dollars on the duvet and leafed through the fake passport made out in the name of Pietro Andrea Bertorelli. Only the photograph was missing. In a side pocket I found the embossing stamp that needed to be used to authenticate the photo. I started counting the money. Beggiato could never have spent it all, even if he did his best. It was enough for a lifetime. I returned the bag to its place. Every night, before I slipped under the covers, I checked that it was there. Around that time, my solitary existence was interrupted by the arrival of another letter. A yellow medium-size padded envelope. The sender was someone called Gianna Tormene. It contained two photographs. They both pictured a woman sitting on a park bench, smiling at the camera. It was Clara, but it took me a while to recognize her. For too many years, her face, even in the sweetest dreams, was the one I saw in agony at the hospital. In the accompanying note, the woman explained she was the mother of a schoolmate of Enrico's. One day they happened to be in the park with the children, and she took the photos for fun. She apologized for not having one of Enrico, but he and her son had started running across the lawns and just then they were far away. She got my address from my lawyer, who was a friend of the family. She decided to send them to me, even though many years had passed. She thought they might give me pleasure.

I framed them and put one in the bedroom, on the night table, and the other in the living room. But I tried not to look at them. The woman wasn't my Clara. Gradually everything became unbearable. The apartment, Heels in a Jiffy, the cemetery, the food from the rosticceria, the wine in the carton, the TV quiz shows. I was getting worse all the time. The darkness that engulfed my mind was rent by flashes of light; Siviero's and his wife's blood turned redder and redder. Valiani and Beggiato became insistent thoughts, difficult to drive away. Sometimes I'd lose my breath and be seized by a panic attack. Afraid that I was losing control, I even went to a specialist. I was very careful in describing the symptoms—and in omitting the truth about what was happening inside my head. Besides, my story was more than enough to convince him I was sick. He prescribed a series of drugs, and right away I started to feel better. Much better. My strength came back, even though my whole life continued to be unbearable. Very soon the specialist was too. Useless, annoying chitchat. One day, at lunch time, I went to the photographer in the supermarket. At home that night I glued one of the four photos in the passport and embossed it with the stamp.

"My name is Pietro Andrea Bertorelli," I said out loud in front of the mirror. One, two, three, twenty times non-stop.

I started to go out with the passport in my pocket. I couldn't be Silvano Contin anymore. One Sunday I happened to see a travel program on TV. Everything else was just a matter of following thoughts and actions in succession. I now live in Fort-de-France on Martinique, and I am Monsieur Pietro Andrea Bertorelli. The darkness still clouds my mind, and the past continues to torment me, but at least I'm a little more calm and aware. I still rely on drugs, but I'm very happy to do so. They allow me to live without hurtling down into the abyss of madness. I must only be careful not to use any alcohol, which could alter the chemical balance that governs my mind. This isn't such a big sacrifice. The French Antilles are famous for rum, but I prefer fried bananas to liquor. Here I'm no longer the man whose wife and son were murdered, and I can look about me without any fear of being recognized. I gaze at the flowers and the gaudy colors of the girls' flimsy dresses. From the terrace of my new house I observe the sunset on the sea. The only emotion I feel is curiosity. Today I'm perfectly aware that I killed two people. I could've avoided it. But it was my right to choose whether or not to forgive. And I haven't forgiven anyone. Not even Beggiato. He thought he'd given me another chance at life by avoiding prison. He might've also thought he was making a noble gesture and squaring accounts. But only in part has he restored what he took away from me.

ABOUT THE AUTHOR

Massimo Carlotto was born in Padua, Italy, and now lives in Sardinia. In addition to the many titles in his extremely popular Alligator series, he is also the author of *The Goodbye Kiss* (Europa Editions, 2006) and *The Fugitive* (Europa Editions, 2007). One of Italy's most popular authors and a major exponent of the Mediterranean Noir novel, Carlotto has been compared with many of the most important American hardboiled crime writers. His novels have been translated into many languages, enjoying enormous success outside of Italy, and several have been made into highly acclaimed films.

AVAILABLE NOW from EUROPA EDITIONS

The Jasmine Isle
Ioanna Karystiani
Fiction - 176 pp - $14.95 - isbn 1-933372-10-9

A modern love story with the force of an ancient Greek tragedy. Set on the spectacular Cycladic island of Andros, *The Jasmine Isle*, one of the finest literature achievements in contemporary Greek, recounts the story of the old sea wolf, Spyros Maltambès, and the beautiful Orsa Saltaferos, sentenced to marry a man she doesn't love and to watch while the man she does love is wed to another.

I Loved You for Your Voice
Sélim Nassib
Fiction - 256 pp - $14.95 - isbn 1-933372-07-9

"Om Kalthoum is great. She really is."—BOB DYLAN

Love, desire, and song set against the colorful backdrop of modern Egypt. The story of Egypt's greatest and most popular singer, Om Kalthoum, told through the eyes of the poet Ahmad Rami, who wrote her lyrics and loved her in vain all his life. This passionate tale of love and longing provides a key to understanding the soul, the aspirations and the disappointments of the Arab world.

The Days of Abandonment
Elena Ferrante
Fiction - 192 pp - $14.95 - isbn 1-933372-00-1

"Stunning . . . The raging, torrential voice of the author is something rare."
—JANET MASLIN, *The New York Times*

"I could not put this novel down. Elena Ferrante will blow you away."
—ALICE SEBOLD, author of *The Lovely Bones*

The gripping story of a woman's descent into devastating emptiness after being abandoned by her husband with two young children to care for.

Cooking with Fernet Branca
James Hamilton-Paterson
Fiction - 288 pp - $14.95 - isbn 1-933372-01-X

"A work of comic genius."—*The Independent*

Gerald Samper, an effete English snob, has his own private hilltop in Tuscany where he whiles away his time working as a ghostwriter for celebrities and inventing wholly original culinary concoctions. Gerald's idyll is shattered by the arrival of Marta, on the run from a crime-riddled former Soviet republic. A series of hilarious misunderstandings brings this odd couple into ever closer and more disastrous proximity.

Old Filth
Jane Gardam
Fiction - 256 pp - $14.95 - isbn 1-933372-13-3

"Jane Gardam's beautiful, vivid and defiantly funny novel is a must."—*The Times*

Sir Edward Feathers has progressed from struggling young barrister to wealthy expatriate lawyer to distinguished retired judge, living out his last days in comfortable seclusion in Dorset. The engrossing and moving account of his life, from birth in colonial Malaya, to Wales, where he is sent as a "Raj orphan," to Oxford, his career and marriage, parallels much of the twentieth century's dramatic history.

Total Chaos
Jean-Claude Izzo
Fiction/Noir - 256 pp - $14.95 - isbn 1-933372-04-4

"Caught between pride and crime, racism and fraternity, tragedy and light, messy urbanization and generous beauty, the city for Montale is a Utopia, an ultimate port of call for exiles. There, he is torn between fatalism and revolt, despair and sensualism."—*The Economist*

This first installment in the legendary *Marseilles Trilogy* sees Fabio Montale turning his back on a police force marred by corruption and racism and taking the fight against the Mafia into his own hands.

The Goodbye Kiss
Massimo Carlotto
Fiction/Noir - 192 pp - $14.95 - isbn 1-933372-05-2

"The best living Italian crime writer."—*Il Manifesto*

An unscrupulous womanizer, as devoid of morals now as he once was full of idealistic fervor, returns to Italy, where he is wanted for a series of crimes. To avoid prison he sells out his old friends, turns his back on his former ideals, and cuts deals with crooked cops. To earn himself the guise of respectability he is willing to go even further, maybe even as far as murder.

Hangover Square
Patrick Hamilton
Fiction/Noir - 280 pp - $14.95 - isbn 1-933372-06-0

"Hamilton is a sort of urban Thomas Hardy: always a pleasure to read, and as social historian he is unparalleled."—NICK HORNBY

Adrift in the grimy pubs of London at the outbreak of World War II, George Harvey Bone is hopelessly infatuated with Netta, a cold, contemptuous small-time actress. George also suffers from occasional blackouts. During these moments one thing is horribly clear: he must murder Netta.

Boot Tracks
Matthew F. Jones
Fiction/Noir - 208 pp - $14.95 - isbn 1-933372-11-7

"Mr. Jones has created a powerful blend of love and violence, of the grotesque and the tender."—*The New York Times*

A commanding, stylishly written novel that tells the harrowing story of an assassination gone terribly wrong and the man and woman who are taking their last chance to find a safe place in a hostile world.

Love Burns
Edna Mazya
Fiction/Noir - 192 pp - $14.95 - isbn 1-933372-08-7

"Starts out as a psychological drama and becomes a strange, funny, unexpected hybrid: a farce thriller. A great book."—*Ma'ariv*

Ilan, a middle-aged professor of astrophysics, discovers that his young wife is having an affair. Terrified of losing her, he decides to confront her lover instead. Their meeting ends in the latter's murder—the unlikely murder weapon being Ilan's pipe—and in desperation, Ilan disposes of the body in the fresh grave of his kindergarten teacher. But when the body is discovered . . .

Departure Lounge
Chad Taylor
Fiction/Noir - 176 pp - $14.95 - isbn 1-933372-09-5

"Entropy noir . . . The hypnotic pull lies in the zigzag dance of its forlorn characters, casting a murky, uneasy sense of doom."—*The Guardian*

A young woman mysteriously disappears. The lives of those she has left behind—family, acquaintances, and strangers intrigued by her disappearance—intersect to form a captivating latticework of coincidences and surprising twists of fate. Urban noir at its stylish and intelligent best.

Minotaur
Benjamin Tammuz
Fiction/Noir - 192 pp - $14.95 - isbn 1-933372-02-8

"A novel about the expectations and compromises that humans create for themselves . . . Very much in the manner of William Faulkner and Lawrence Durrell."—*The New York Times*

An Israeli secret agent falls hopelessly in love with a young English girl. Using his network of contacts and his professional expertise, he takes control of her life without ever revealing his identity. *Minotaur* is a complex and utterly original story about a solitary man driven from one side of Europe to the other by his obsession.

Dog Day
Alicia Giménez-Bartlett
Fiction/Noir - 208 pp - $14.95 - isbn 1-933372-14-1

"Giménez-Bartlett has discovered a world full of dark corners and hidden elements."—*ABC*

In this hardboiled fiction for dog lovers and lovers of dog mysteries, detective Petra Delicado and her maladroit sidekick, Garzon, investigate the murder of a tramp whose only friend is a mongrel dog named Freaky. One murder leads to another and Delicado finds herself involved in the sordid, dangerous world of fight dogs. *Dog Day* is first-rate entertainment.

Carte Blanche
Carlo Lucarelli
Fiction/Noir - 120 pp - $14.95 - isbn 1-933372-15-X

"Carlo Lucarelli is the great promise of Italian crime writing."—*La Stampa*

April 1945, Italy. Commissario De Luca is heading up a dangerous investigation into the private lives of the rich and powerful during the frantic final days of the fascist republic. The hierarchy has guaranteed De Luca their full cooperation, so long as he arrests the "right" suspect. The house of cards built by Mussolini in the last months of WWII is collapsing and De Luca faces a world mired in sadistic sex, dirty money, drugs and murder.

The Big Question
Wolf Erlbruch
Children's Illustrated Fiction - 52 pp - $14.95 - isbn 1-933372-03-6

Named Best Book at the 2004 Children's Book Fair in Bologna.

A stunningly beautiful and poetic illustrated book for children that poses the biggest of all big questions: Why am I here? A chorus of voices—including the cat's, the baker's, the pilot's and the soldier's—offers us some answers. But nothing is certain, except that as we grow each one of us will pose the question differently and be privy to different answers.

The Butterfly Workshop
Wolf Erlbruch
Children's Illustrated Fiction - 40 pp - $14.95 - isbn 1 933372-12-5

For children and adults alike: Odair, one of the "Designers of All Things" and grandson of the esteemed inventor of the rainbow, has been banished to the insect laboratory as punishment for his overactive imagination. But he still dreams of one day creating a cross between a bird and a flower. Then, after a helpful chat with a dog . . .